Don't Stand Still

A NOVEL BY

JoAnn Scanlon

ISBN-13: **978-1515158288**

ISBN-10: **1515158284**

Library of Congress Control Number: **2015911599**

LCCN Imprint Name: **CreateSpace Independent Publishing Platform, North Charleston, SC**

Don't Stand Still

I wanted to express my gratitude to my family and friends who encouraged me to follow my dream of writing a book. To my little boys, who inspire me every day, I love you with all my heart. To my parents, whom I will always look up to, I miss you and love you always.

Acknowledgments

I'm truly grateful for the many people who are in my life today and those who have passed on and yet left an incredible light in my life. My mom…I don't think I can say enough passionate words to describe her wonderful qualities. I thank my mother for her compassion and endearing love through everything. She was the go-to person for her children, grandchildren, siblings, and friends for advice, support, and empathy. She taught me how to be strong against any challenges that come. Although my mother passed from cancer, she will forever hold a place in my heart. I also want to express my gratitude to my father for celebrating life every day and living it to the fullest. He taught us to laugh and to enjoy what we have, putting those he loved in front of himself and striving to provide the best life possible for his family. My father passed from cancer as well, but I know they are both watching over us. Without my parents, I wouldn't have the gracious appreciation and appetite for life that I have today.

Thank you to my brother, Geno, an excellent father, brother, supportive uncle, and a man my parents would be proud of. Thank you, Geno, for making me laugh. Thank you to my sister Lisa, an excellent mother just like my mother was. Her love for her family radiates off her. Thank you, Lisa, for being a role model, inspiring mom, awesome sister, wonderful aunt, and a great friend. My sister Gail, you are as wonderful as they come. You keep us all together as the communicator, always making sure everyone is OK. You got those qualities from our parents, and I am so proud to say you are my sister. Thank you for fighting against the challenges in your life and turning out to be an incredible aunt, dedicated sister, and great friend.

I would also like to say thank you to three other important people in my life. Without these individuals, I would not be where I am today. Thank you to my husband, Kevin, for coming into my life years ago. Kevin is a strong-willed, goal-oriented, and supportive partner who helps me plan my career and personal life.

Don't Stand Still

He has taught me to set goals in making my dreams realities. Thank you for my past, my present, and my future. Thank you, Kevin. I am not sure you even know how your role in my life has changed me. I am also appreciative for my boys, Nicolas and Tyler. They both fill my heart with pure love. Hearing their laughter puts a smile on my face; hearing them cry puts tears in my eyes. I am grateful to have them in my life to care for, to love, and to be a role model for them. I want to teach them that they can do anything they want as long as they try; it may not be what they expected the first time around, but they can try again to improve.

I also want to thank an incredible woman in my professional life: Adele Suddes. She has believed in me throughout the years and has always taught me that I could be whoever I wanted to be and always reminded me that I need to be happy in what I am doing on a day-to-day basis. Thank you, Adele, for being a great manager, admired mentor, compassionate friend, and supporter of my dreams.

My list of individuals to whom I am grateful can go on

endlessly. I am thankful for my entire family including my nieces and nephews, aunts and uncles, and cousins. For Allison Manning who inquired each day about the status of my book, who motivated me to finish, who encouraged me that I could do it, who helped with my website and the cover of my books—thank you! For Dann Dufresne who stayed up late to assist with formatting my manuscript – thank you!

My friends who help me appreciate each day of my life, thank you. For those individuals who believed in me, told me to follow my dream, and encouraged me, I send my warmest gratitude to you all.

<u>Prologue</u>

The Past

Don't Stand Still

I love you, isn't that enough?

—Michael

Chapter 1

Falling Deep

Stephanie opened her eyes, enjoying the feel of Michael's sheets wrapped around her bare body. She turned to wish him a good morning but his half of the bed was empty. Sitting up in a panic, Stephanie yelled his name.

It was quiet in his apartment except for the sound of music. She tried to listen for him talking on the phone or simply being muffled by the music that was playing. She closed her eyes listening to the sounds of their morning but didn't seem to hear his voice anywhere. Focusing on the music, Stephanie finally made out the words to the song, *The lady in red is dancing with me cheek to cheek, There's nobody here, it's just you and me, it's*

Don't Stand Still

where I wanna be, But I hardly know this beauty by my side, I'll never forget the way you look tonight. Just as she sat up to search for him, Michael galantly strolled into the room holding a red, sexy dress–just as vibrant as the smile on his face.

Still bundled in his sheets, Stephanie slid her way over to Michael on the bed. He softly placed the dress on the comforter, "Do you like it?"

This man was Stephanie's world. "You are so theatrical! I'm starting to think I'm a barbie doll you're dressing up. I love it, but where am I going to wear that to? It's kind of short." She reached over to the end table to grab a t-shirt. About to put it on, Michael reached for it and threw it to the floor. "What are you doing? I need to get dressed."

He gave her those eyes that made her melt each time, "Will you try it on? You can wear it tonight when we meet everyone." He slipped it off the hanger and ripped off the tag.

Don't Stand Still

Stephanie gasped, "Why did you rip the tags off? This may not even fit me. You are one crazy man." She kissed him then took the dress.

She had never been insecure in front of him naked; which was always suprising to her since she wasnt completely happy with the way her body looked. It didn't matter to Michael though—he made her feel beautiful every day.

Michael sat perched on the bed watching her trying to slip into the dress. He was in plaid boxer shorts and shirtless, the ideal look Stephanie loved cuddling up with. "I think I know your size by now. I felt every part of your body, I know your curves. I know your height."

Stephanie stepped into the dress. It was very form fitting to her body.; however the length was shorter than she normally would wear. "It's kind of short, honey." She didn't like dressing in a seductive way when they went out with a group of friends. It wasn't offensive to them but always drew stares from bystanders, which always put Michael on edge. Stephanie could handle his flaws of course, but didn't want close friends to notice his insecurities.

"You look beautiful. Sexy. Mine." He leaped out of bed, and walked out of the room leaving her standing there. The music began to play again, this time from the beginning. "May I have this dance?", e said as he walked into the room, holding out his hand to her.

How did I get so lucky to find a man like this at a carnival? Stephanie thought. They danced together till the song was over. As the music slowed to a mellow end, Michael unzipped Stephanie's dress,picked her up and placed her gently on the bed. "I love you."

***

Stephanie was straightening her hair as she yelled out to Michael. "I don't know why we have to stay at a hotel tonight when you have a bed of your own." She was brushing her hair as he stood behind her. "Red shirt huh? I'm taking it that wasn't a coincidence. We are one fashionable couple." She turned around to kiss him.

Michael unplugged her iron, took the brush and brushed the back of her hair. "I want us to have a fun night tonight without worrying about driving home. I think that is the responsible idea we all had."

He opened the bathroom cabinet and took out some hair products to finish off his look. Stephanie laughed, "I think you put more chemicals in your hair than I do!"

Michael responded, "It's tough to be me."

The phone ringing interrupted their conversation. Stephanie walked away to take her call, "Hey you, yes, we are almost ready. Are you heading there now?"

Robert, her best friend, was on the phone, "Yes. Carla and the others are already there. Did you make reservations? I'm starving. It's going to be a calm night of dinner, drinks and dancing, right?" Robert had spoke to Stephanie in the past about the arguments her and Michael has publicly had before. It always made him uncomfortable.

"It's going to be fun. Reservations have been made, it's under Ferrari. Can't wait to see you. Love you." She hung up the phone. Michael stood next to her, straight faced.

"I thought you only loved me." Michael teased her. "Let's head out I don't want to keep everyone waiting."

Stephanie went into the bedroom to shut off the light. Grabbing her purse and tucking away her phone and lipstick, Stephanie turned to look for the overnight bag she had packed earlier. As she rummaged through the bed and closet, she couldn't seem to find where she had placed it. She was getting angry at herself for always forgetting things.

Michael couldn't help but laugh as he watched her walked

into the living room all flustered, "I have it on my shoulder, you silly." She walked over and playfully hit him.

"You were making me think I was crazy, thanks a lot." Stephanie laughed at herself.

The car drive to the restaurant was quiet. Stephanie was in deep thought, *I hope this is a good night tonight*. What Robert said on the phone had made her second guess it. Dinner at the hotel restaurant, karaoke at the bar then dancing at the club. Stephanie thought, *it's going to be fine. It will be a drama free night.*

Her thoughts were interrupted by Michael's touch. He placed his hand on her knee. "We are here. What were you thinking about? Looked as if you were in another world. A world away from me." He lifted her hand up, kissed each finger. "You and I forever."

"I was just thinking about what a great night we are all going to have. I see them all inside. Let's go." She opened her car door then stepped out. The valet took Michael's keys. Walking towards the restaurant, Stephanie was startled by Michael's reach.

Michael was confused as to why she was so tense, "Why did you jump like that? Here you forgot your purse in the car. Wait up for your date babe!"

Stephanie was embarrassed as she turned to him, "I'm sorry. Thanks for becoming my memory, I've been so spacey lately. I would have realized it was in the car in the second we got in there. I don't know why I jumped, I think I'm just anxious to get in."

They both walked hand in hand as Robert came over. He shook Michael's hand then turned to Stephanie to hug and kiss her. "You look hot in that red dress! The table is over here. I ordered you a glass of wine. Michael, I wasn't sure which beer you wanted. The cocktail waitress said she will be over in a few minutes."

Don't Stand Still

There was a group of ten of them sitting at the table. Stephanie sipped at her glass of wine while others were on their second and third beverages. Dinner plates were being cleared off the table. The thing coming to the table was shots for everyone, except Stephanie. She handed hers off to Robert who then handed it off to Michael. Stephanie gave Robert a nasty glare.

Stephanie excused herself to go to the restroom. As she walked the path to the ladies room she felt the stares she was receiving. She knew that only meant one thing. *It's not my fault, he put me in this dress.*

Stephanie cleared her head for a few minutes. She then pushed open the door and not to her surprise, was greeted by Michael. "Everything ok in there?"

"Yes, I'm good. Did I miss anything exciting?" Stephanie figured it would be easier to keep the conversation going while they were walking back to the table.

Don't Stand Still

Stephanie heard the words she dreaded to hear, "Got a problem man?" She grabbed Michael's arm and pulled him away from an gawky man staring at Stephanie.

She gave the man a slight smile, then kissed Michael on the cheek. "Come on, honey." She was able to pull him away from the situation but was afraid to look Robert's way.

Stephanie was tense—her shoulders pressed tight and back clenched; she knew she needed another drink. Walking back to her friends, Stephanie tried to break the ice of the group. "Who's up first? I think it should be Carla." Carla shook her head. Her friends all tried to get Carla up but it was always unsuccessful.

The night turned into a genuine night of laughs and cheers. As the night went on, Stephanie began to forget about the incident earlier and enjoyed watching Robert and Michael cheering each other on. She stared at them in awe, the two men in her life.

Michael, figgity and energetic, left the crowd for the DJ

booth and on his way back was stopped by Carla. "What are you going to sing?" she asked, his response was sarcastic as usual, "You'll see my lady."

Michael enjoyed conversations with Carla. They both had the same sense of humor—dry and witty, always mocking situations and people around them

Stephanie tried not to pay too much attention to their conversation. While she did want to give Michael the space to talk to other people, she more or less wanted quality time to speak with Robert. Robert and Stephanie have known each other for many years and had developed quite an honest and judgement free relationship. He spilled his evening before while Stephanie carefully listened to each detail. The conversation was getting good until she heard the announcer call, "Michael Pellegrino to the stage please!".

Stephanie knew she needed to end the conversation she was having with Robert, for now. As she looked over to the stage,

Don't Stand Still

Michael was handed the microphone. He started off softly, *"Oh. my love, my darling, I've hungered for your touch."* As the lyrics went on Michael became more confident and obnoxious. Staring at Stephanie, Michael fell to his knees, *"Are you still mine? I need your love. I need your love. God speed your love to me."*

Everyone cheered for him, for the two "happily in love" people. She stood up and kissed him as he walked off the stage. He was alittle uneasy on his feet, so they both walked over to the table but noticed everyone was getting ready to leave.

Robert was the first to speak, "Let's head over across the hall to dance. You guys checked in earlier today, right?"

Michael was leaning on her, "Yup, we're all checked in. We're good for the night!"

The music was extremely loud in the venue. Stephanie tried to ask Michael if he was okay but every time she leaned over to whisper in his ear he kissed her. While Stephanie ordered water,

Don't Stand Still

Michael headed back to the bar for a beer.

Robert reached out to take Stephanie's hand along with Carla. "Come on girls! Let's go dance. Michael will meet up with us on the dance floor."

The three of them danced four songs together. Carefree and wild, Stephanie found herself swaying to the music and enjoying the action with her friends. After the second song, Stephanie had stopped looking to Michael for approval—she retracted her concern and danced for herself. As Robert twirled Carla then Stephanie then Carla again, Stephanie's smile continued to grow; she was truly having a great night.

Growing tired from the dancing, Robert, Carla and Stephanie walked back to the table but couldn't seem to spot Michael. Asking others where he went, no one seemd to have any idea.

Robert put his hand on Stephanie's shoulder, "He's not

going to just disappear, Steph. He'll come back. He's not gone."
Robert didn't know where Michael went either but he was just
trying to comfort her.

"Ugh, where did he go?", Stephanie asked Robert,
exhausted and irritated. "I walked around this place three times, in
and out of crowds, but I don't see him any where." She took out
her phone and tried to call him again. No answer. One more time.
Still nothing. Everyone was starting to leave so Stephanie grabbed
for her purse and walked towards the exit with Carla and Robert
following her.

Carla spoke first, "What do you want to do? Do you want
to stay in my room with me?"

Robert interrupted, "Are you kidding with me? If he ever
went back to the room and she never showed up, he would go
room to room knocking on doors."

Carla sounded defensive, "I'm only trying to help. Do you

16

have any better ideas?"

Stephanie stood there as Robert and Carla bantered with one another. Finally, Stephanie spoke up, "Please, stop it." She opened her purse to grab for her hotel key. "I'm just gonna go to my room and wait for him."

Robert walked by her side, "I'll go with you. After I check your room out I'll leave, but I'll have my phone on all night. Please call me when he finally comes to the room."

Carla's room was three doors away from Stephanie's. They said good night to one another and Robert walked Stephanie to her door. It was late and they were both tired so Stephanie lazily unlocked her door and fumbled through the entrance. Robert paved the way for Stephanie to look for Michael again—he checked out the bedroom, no sign, then looked on the patio, still nothing, and finally retreated back to the middle of the hotel room. Stephanie, growing with panic and worry, was seemingly drawn to the bathroom—as if Michael was calling out to her. And there he was, plopped in the bathtub, sitting in his clothes and sipping on a beer. Stephanie just looked at him and smiled. She was happy to find him but not happy that he was alone.

She walked out of the bathroom to find Robert. "Thanks, for walking me here. I'm fine now." She pointed to the bathoom door to get the point across that he was safe. "I'll call you tomorrow."

Stephanie walked into the bathroom and looked down at Michael as he took his next sip of his beer. She took the bottle from his hand and poured the rest of it out. Stepping into the tub, Stephanie sat down ready to confront her boyfriend's state. "Are you alright?"

Michael, drunk and slobbery, responded. "I love you. Can you please take off that dress? Please. I love you."

Stephanie did as she was told. "I love you, too. What can I do to help you?" She was feeling the need to cover up. "Let's go

18

into the bed, I can help you up."

"Why can't it be just you and I?", Michael wined, "I love the relationship we have. What we have is perfect." Michael expressed his feelings but Stephanie couldn't take him seriously sitting in a bathroom tub.

"It *is* just you and I honey. I don't want anyone but you. Come with me." Stephanie stood up and reached for his hand. She realized how much help he really did need. She lifted one of his arms and walked him into the bedroom. Placing him on the bed, Michael fell back sinking into the pillow. Heading back to the bathroom to brush her teeth, Stephanie put on a bathrobe and shut the light. By the time she came back to the bedroom, Michael was passed out. She took off his shoes and unbuttoned his shirt; it was all that she could do.

The buzz of her phone went off and when she looked down at the display, she saw that it was a text from Robert, *are you ok?*

Don't Stand Still

Stephanie responded – *everything is fine, he's asleep. Good night.*

Shutting off her phone, Stephanie drifted into a deep desparing sleep.

***

The next morning was a groggy Sunday wakeup so Stephanie and Michael decided to go shopping. Stephanie bought some clothes, Michael bought some sports memoborlia and the two had a nice relaxing lunch together. They had never spoken of the night before throughout the whole day. As they drove back home, both Stephanie and Michael were in good spirits.

"All this back and forth to your apartment, I should just move in. But that can't happen till someone makes the next move. Ahem." Stephanie sarcastically pestered Michael.

Either Michael didn't hear what Stephanie said or he didn't want to comment; Michael stayed quiet until they parked the car.

"Did you want to go home first or do you have enough clothes for one more night?" he asked.

"I'm good." Stephanie was confused as to why he didn't respond. Stephanie thought, *that would be the next step for us, marriage.* "Am I getting that you don't want to marry me. You're quiet every time your parents or I bring it up. Why?"

He turned to her as he opened the door to his apartment, "Let's get in." He opened the door for her. "I love you, isn't that enough? I love what we have in one another. We are spontaneous and carefree and passionate. Our love for one another is stronger than some of the marriages out there."

Stephanie heard fear in his voice, "Is that what it is, are you afraid? Nothing will change between us."

"If nothing will change between us then we don't need a piece of paper telling us we love one another." Michael was obviously tense about the topic.

Don't Stand Still

That night, Stephanie laid fast asleep in Michael's arms. Awakened by his touch, Stephanie opened her eyes and saw him staring while he caressed her face. Without speaking, he sat up and removed his shirt. He grabbed her hand and put it on his heart. He kissed each finger and then leaned down and kissed her lightly on each cheek.

"I love you, Stephanie," he whispered. They had made love before, but this was different. He stared deeply into her eyes without speaking a word. They couldn't possibly be any closer than they were that night. Michael and Stephanie didn't have to try; they just fit like a pair of gloves. They fell asleep in each other's arms, never letting go until the morning.

***

Two months later, Michael didn't answer his cell phone. After a few calls went unanswered, Stephanie decided to go to his apartment but when she arrived, he wasn't there. She walked into his bedroom but the bed was made as if it hadn't been slept in for days. His closet door, slightly creaked, caught her eye but when she opened it fully, everything was gone. His clothes, shoes, suits—gone.

In disbelief, Stephanie shuffled into the living room. All the albums of them were gone. They were always on the couch table, easily within reach. Flustered and on the verge of endless tears, Stephanie spotted a note in it's place.

"I'm sorry, Stephanie." He was gone.

Part One

The Present

Don't Stand Still

You can't dwell on one person who broke your heart.

—Carla

Chapter 2

Holding On

Stephanie Ferrari lived in a small populated area not too far from her friends or family. She chose this location because it was close to all the people she cared about. She liked things small and simple, and that was what this home represented to her.

For Stephanie, the small things mattered the most. The weather and her deck were two of those minor things. The deck was dependable, but the weather had its moments. She didn't have the energy to focus on anything that involved decisions. The security of knowing that her deck would be there for her morning or night, sunshine or rain, was what she needed at this time—dependability.

The deck was her favorite part of the condo. On some

evenings, she ate her dinner out there and then went for a run on the beach. Those were the most relaxing nights she could remember. One Thursday night after work, she decided to complete her run before dinner. She then sat on the beach to reflect on her past. Three hours later, the moon was shining down on her, and she realized she hadn't eaten dinner.

Stephanie always enjoyed the month of August. The weather was as she preferred it—warm, with a slight breeze at night. She loved the way the breeze touched her face, almost the way *he* used to caress her from her cheek to her chin. She enjoyed the stars that lit up the sky, almost the way he used to make her feel all lit up inside. Stephanie lay on her lounge chair, visioning herself sitting between his legs, with her head on his chest and his arms wrapped around her, holding her tightly. She recalled how she lifted her head up, turned around, and looked at him, and he kissed her on the nose.

Stephanie thought, *I need to move on.* But the memories were still so fresh. She wanted to hold on to every touch, every feeling, and every memory.

For the most part, she was a loner, with the exception of Robert. He was the stability in her life. Stephanie loved him with every ounce of herself. She needed come to terms with this relationship and her future.

***

It was Saturday, the best day of the week to Stephanie. She could sleep late and then take a book out to the deck to enjoy the rest of her morning outside. Her living arrangements were perfect for her needs. The condo was perfect not only because of the size, but also because of her passion for the outdoors. Stephanie started her Saturday mornings sitting outside with her morning coffee. She used the time to reflect on her week, which usually included work, running errands, and spending time with Robert.

This morning, Stephanie watched the neighbor's children playing outside. It made her think of her childhood. She loved school. She asked the teachers to give her extra work to do during the summer. The teachers laughed and handed her extra work sheets. Some of her friends played dolls, but Stephanie wanted to play school. She took on the role of schoolteacher, of course.

When she began high school, she received the summer reading list and read the mandatory books and all of the optional ones as well. Her goal was to always be prepared for any conversation in the classroom. She read them because she felt that she needed to academically, but she also read them because she loved to get lost in books. She never considered herself an overachiever; she just wanted to do it all. Stephanie didn't enjoy the time when she had nothing to do. She always had to keep moving and doing something. Teachers and friends were concerned about her and thought she possibly had attention deficit disorder.

As an adult, Stephanie felt good knowing that she overcame any challenges in her past and became a successful businesswoman.

The funny fact about her earlier years, which carried into

her qualities as an adult, is that she always loved drama (usually not the good drama). Stephanie was like the dog chasing the fire truck as it passed. If an accident happened nearby, she wanted to go to it. When she was a child, she was frightened to see someone injured on the ground from an accident, but something pulled her to the scene. After the emergency vehicles drove away and the crowd dispersed, Stephanie took pictures of the sidewalk or area and attempted to write a story about the incident. Back then, she didn't have a computer. She put the picture on the front page and wrote by hand what she believed happened. Robert, her childhood friend, told her how he cringed every time he heard a siren because he knew she was on her way to the scene—most of the time with him by her side.

Robert Rossi and Stephanie had been friends since kindergarten. He only went by the name of Robert. Not Rob and not Robbie. No one close to him was allowed to call him anything but Robert. He said that when he was born he was given that name, and that's how he wanted people to address him. Robert was a formal person from childhood to adulthood. Stephanie never went against him. As always, she respected his choices.

When they first met at the age of five, they played games together, shared their toys, and laughed like crazy together. Even as adults, they did the same thing, except for playing with children's toys.

From attending early schooling together to working at the same company, Stephanie couldn't picture her life without Robert.

In many ways, Robert was Stephanie's soul mate: as children they adventured into a made up detective club, pursued imaginary cases and balanced each other's curiosity with realism. However there was one slight halt on their future: Stephanie was into men and so was Robert.

Stephanie asked, "Why do you think someone left this candy wrapper on the ground? There has to be a reason. Could the person be nearby? Do you think someone has been kidnapped?" She believed that actions and words always had meanings.

Don't Stand Still

Robert responded, "They're lazy, ignorant children who don't care about our environment. They enjoyed the candy bar and tossed the wrapper on the ground."

Even though Robert and Stephanie had known each other for practically their whole lives, they always had something to talk about. Last week, they sat outside together having a few drinks and asking each other questions they probably knew the answers to but enjoyed the quizzing anyway.

"What's your favorite color?" Stephanie asked.

He responded, "Blue," which she should have known since that was the only color he wore. "Who's your favorite author?"

She didn't believe he knew the answer, since they read different types of books. "James Patterson and Nicholas Sparks." She alternated in her reading from suspense to love stories. That way, she got her adrenaline pumping with the suspense book and then got the romantic side of her out with the next book. She loved getting lost in a book and becoming the characters in the novel.

Don't Stand Still

The questioning went on till one in the morning, and then they went inside and went to sleep. They had sleepovers on an alternating schedule. One weekend, he stayed at her house, and the next, she stayed at his. It worked for them most of the time.

***

The phone rang and woke Stephanie up from her daydream. She picked up the phone, and immediately regretted it. It was Carla.

Carla Kadans had everything—the looks, the career, the personality, and the popularity. Her confidence overflowed. She never needed to fret about anyone or anything. If she didn't have something, she didn't need it.

Carla and Stephanie were friends for a few years but recently drifted apart. Carla didn't agree with Stephanie's lifestyle, and Stephanie didn't enjoy defending herself or her actions every time they spoke.

"Hi, honey! How have you been? Are you with Robert this

morning?" Carla asked. Carla and Robert got along well, but Carla continuously told Stephanie she needed to go out with just the girls more often. Carla accepted Robert and Stephanie's friendship, but still pressured Stephanie to live life and enjoy the nightlife on the weekends. Carla thought Robert was holding Stephanie back from finding Mr. Right. *Is there such a thing?* Stephanie wondered.

Stephanie responded with as much positive energy as she could pump up. "Things are going OK. I'm enjoying the weather. I'm watching my neighbor's children chase after one another. It's the funniest thing, watching the older one run in fear from his younger brother." She laughed. "Robert will be here later this afternoon. He had an appointment this morning. Why, what are your plans for the day?" Stephanie regretted the question because she knew, as always, it would end with an invitation that she would have to reject. Her excuses were running thin, but Carla never gave up on her. That's what friends were for.

"I'm going to go through my clothes today to see what I

need to buy for the fall. I was hoping we could spend the day together. We can start by going shopping and then grab a bite to eat. Maybe we can even go out dancing afterward. I don't mind driving if you want me to pick you up."

Stephanie thought Carla knew what her answer would be, especially since Robert was coming over. She took her time to respond to give Carla the satisfaction that she was considering the possibility. Honesty was always the best route. "I would love to go shopping with you, but Robert will be here this afternoon. And regarding the nightlife, I'm just not ready for that right now. You know I'm just getting over my last relationship. Everyone knows how hard it's been for me. I need to take time for myself, and I really don't enjoy going into crowds. Don't be upset. Just say you understand, please."

"Take time for yourself, or take time for you and Robert? Robert will never give you what you need. He is your friend, not your prince." Carla sighed. "You can't dwell on one person who broke your heart. Yes, it was tough, but move on. It was tough watching you go through it. Do you think he's thinking about you? Do you think he stopped living? We knew him. He loved life too much to not enjoy it. I'm trying to help you by taking you out to move on. What is Robert doing to help you get over this?" Her tone was now as agitated as Stephanie was about her harassing her to go out.

Stephanie felt herself get defensive but tried to remain calm. She believed that Robert did help her deal with what happened to her. He understood she wanted to talk about the past and about the present but with no intention to discuss the future. He didn't pressure her to do anything that she wasn't ready for but was her ears when she needed them or his shoulder to cry on. Robert held her up as she was crashing down. There was no other way to explain it except that Robert was her rock. It was tough for Stephanie to listen to Carla accusing Robert of not helping her through the toughest time of her life.

So she made probably the worst mistake she had made in a long time. She just didn't want to deal with the confrontation, and the words flowed out with hardly any emotion attached to them. "How about Robert and I meet you for dinner? Then we'll discuss the possibility of going out afterward." She had every intention of going home after dinner.

"Great! This is so exciting. I'll call you later this afternoon to discuss where we should go. This will be fun even for Robert, I promise. I'll meet you at your house at seven. It's about time you put the Michael situation past you."

Stephanie thought Carla said his name without truly meaning harm, but hearing that name again brought back the anger, the hurt, and definitely the anxiety. His name shot through her heart like a burning pitchfork. Michael Pellegrino, her one-true soul mate.

Don't Stand Still

Drink up, honey. Now, can you please talk to me, not at

me?

—Robert

Chapter 3

Stepping Out

Stephanie attempted to forget about the phone call by cleaning her house. She knew Carla was right, and she needed to move on. Her heart said otherwise. The heartache was still there, but the anger had drifted away. She hoped the night would be good for her.

But now was the time for cleaning. Stephanie had a process in anything she did. There was even a process for cleaning. She cleaned one room, and once the entire room was clean, she lit a candle. It was a cleansing experience. Her last step was to update her spreadsheet that listed all the rooms with a checklist of what needed to be done daily, weekly, and monthly. It felt good to check something off. Something she started should have a finish.

Don't Stand Still

Stephanie thought, *You don't walk away from something you haven't finished, whether it's cleaning a room or starting a relationship. Don't walk away till you make it final with a checkmark in the box.*

Stephanie finished cleaning her house and then started to think about her conversation with Carla. Maybe Carla had the right idea to go through her wardrobe to see what she needed for the fall. Stephanie went through her pants and realized she had a mass of black items. Black work pants, black sweat pants, and even outdated black jeans. She counted eight black blazers, twelve pairs of black work pants, and four pairs of black heels. Everyone at work kept telling her she needed more color in her wardrobe and that she was dressing for a funeral every day. She thought this statement was definitely not true. Wearing black made her look more sophisticated and professional. It didn't mean she was possibly depressed over a relationship that went bad out of the blue. *Right?*

Just then, the front door opened. It could only be one

person.

"Hey, honey, I'm home!" Then a short pause. "Hello? Where are you?" Robert yelled out to her.

Stephanie was still cleaning out her closet. "I'm up in my bedroom. Come up and join in the fun."

She heard him in her kitchen getting something to drink. She thought, *I hope he's not dripping any soda or anything on my counters that I just cleaned.* She wouldn't dare say this to him because it would bring out the OCD conversation she hated having with him. She could be relaxed about it, or at least act relaxed and not high-strung.

Robert walked in the room and leaned over to kiss Stephanie's cheek. "OK, what's with all the cleaning? I see you've completed all the rooms, or shall I say I smell that you have cleaned."

The scents of apple-cider and vanilla candles burned through the house. The smell of clean rooms put a smile on

Don't Stand Still

Stephanie's face.

"What could have upset you from the time I spoke with you earlier this morning till now?" He remained in the doorway of her bedroom.

"I don't need to be upset to clean my house. Dust gathers, laundry has to be done, and, every once in a while, the bathrooms need to be cleaned." She tried not to be sarcastic, but she was emotionally drained today. She noticed his hands were hidden behind his back. "What do you have behind your back? I'm not into surprises today."

Robert's face went from smiling to concerned. He handed her a drink and then sat down on the bed. He had made both of them mimosas and probably had a pitcher of them downstairs. "Drink up, honey. Now, can you please talk *to* me, and not *at* me? What's bothering you? If you want to talk about it now, we can, or if you prefer, we can just go for a walk. It's your choice. No pressure."

Don't Stand Still

This was why she loved Robert so much. He gave her the space she needed and didn't harass her about anything. Stephanie knew he cared about her and wanted to know what was going on, but, at the same time, he knew she would talk to him when she was ready. Their relationship was perfect.

"Are you OK?" Robert pushed some of her clothes to the side of her bed and sat down.

She finished hanging up the clothes she decided to keep and took a large gulp of her drink. She told Robert that she wanted to go for a walk. They went downstairs and blew out all the candles.

Stephanie grabbed a sweater and her keys. "Wait. Are you hungry? Do you want to pack a lunch, so we can eat on the beach?" She went to the kitchen, grabbed a cooler, and started to pack some snacks. Robert took out the bread to make chicken-salad sandwiches. They finished their drinks and put the pitcher in the fridge for later.

Don't Stand Still

As Stephanie locked the door, she thought, *How am I supposed to bring this up to Robert without getting upset, or, worse, getting Robert upset?* They walked down the path to the beach, which was less than ten minutes away. Stephanie stopped to take her shoes off. She loved the feeling of sand in her toes.

She looked over at Robert in his fashionable sunglasses, dark tan, and just-right hair. He fit the picture of tall, dark, and handsome. Too bad he couldn't be her tall, dark, and handsome prince, but she was flattered to have him as her other half in other ways.

When they reached their destination, they put down their chairs and the cooler. Stephanie needed a few minutes alone to think the conversation through before she opened up to talk with him. "Do you mind if I go for a fast run before we eat and talk?" She recently started to work out, which improved her state of mind tremendously. She enjoyed running and doing classes at the gym. She felt this was her time to get healthier, and it was something she needed to do for herself. It was the first year she was not embarrassed to wear shorts. Working out helped her emotionally, mentally, and physically.

Stephanie ran down the beach to determine what was really bothering her. Her pace increased as she thought. Was it moving forward, or was it facing her past? Her feelings on her past were constantly conflicted. She was happy that she had a love so great but was angry that it ended so abruptly. She thought back to the breakup, and what had, unfortunately, happened to her postbreakup. She thought the blame rested on no one but her. If she was to move forward, that meant she had to file away what she should have done, what she could have done, and what she would have done differently. She knew there would never be a love that compared to what she had experienced.

She believed her future was now a dead end. She thought, *If I know that no one will ever compare to him and to us, why move forward? Why waste the time? There is only one soul mate for each person.*

Stephanie returned to their chairs. She leaned down to grab

a bottle of water. Robert checked out the scenery as half-naked bodies walked by. He believed that if he wore sunglasses, he could stare at anyone. It was funny when people shot nasty glances at him. He always looked like he had no idea why they were looking at him in disgust.

"Do you really think you're being sneaky? They can see your eyes right through those lenses." At least she had a chuckle over that.

"I'm watching the seagull over there. That's it." He handed her a sandwich from the cooler as she sat down next to him. They sat in total silence, watching the waves—at least that's what she was watching.

Stephanie moved her feet in the sand, enjoying her sandwich. She glanced over at Robert and tried to decide if this could be it. Robert and Stephanie were in sync in everything. Everything seemed so comfortable and so right. They met most of their needs. They were friends who would always love one another but were not in love with each other.

Don't Stand Still

"I've decided to go out with Carla tonight. I've also decided to take you with me as my date, if you'll accept, my darling." She laughed. "We're going out for dinner, and then we can make an excuse to come back to my place. I've chosen a few movies we can watch. I believe it was my choice next." The plan seemed like a good one. They needed to eat; they enjoyed the same movies, and quality alone time for them and a pitcher of mimosas at the house to finish.

"Carla wants us, or, shall I say, wants you to go out dancing after dinner. Steph, I agree with her. You need to go out. I'm happy to be your date tonight. Since you're ready to go out, does this mean you're ready to discuss what happened with your relationship with Mike?"

She wasn't.

"Your life is good right now. You are finally happy with yourself. You have a great career. You're back to your confident self. Most of all, you finally have your health back. I love everything about you, but I don't want you to spend the rest of your life with just me. It's not fair to you. I want you to share yourself with someone who can give you what you deserve." He held her hands and stared into her eyes. "You know how much I love you, don't you?"

Tears filled Stephanie's eyes, but she knew she needed to hear this. They were the words that would set her off on her final rampage. "I know, Robert, and I love you too. But I'm not happy. I may be living my life, moving forward step-by-step, but happiness is not where I'd say I am. I did have someone I wanted to share my life with. Do you forget that? He was everything to me—my sun, moon, and stars. I couldn't breathe when I wasn't with him. We had a love that I've never even seen in the movies because ours was better. Even though he hurt me in the worst way, I miss him every day." She knew how wrong she sounded, but she truly believed that she and Michael were born to be with one another.

Robert took a deep breath before carefully responding to her. "You're right. He was everything to you. I don't doubt that. But he left you. Remember, where I found you? I found you on his floor, curled up, crying. You had a nervous breakdown because of this breakup. He may have given you all the love in the world that continues to fill your heart, but he also gave you heartache. He's been gone for almost a year. No contact with you at all. You know he's aware of what happened to you afterward. If he was your prince, your fairytale, shouldn't he have called you?"

Robert put his hand on her knee, and, with his other hand, he turned her face toward him. Tears flowed down her face. "Honey, lets take a different tactic. Tell me your story, yours and Mike's. Start from the beginning and tell me how it ended." Robert knew most of these details, but it had been so long since Stephanie was able to speak about the good memories. She began telling their story.

Don't Stand Still

I want you forever in my life.

—Michael

Chapter 4

Reliving It

Stephanie took a deep breath and thought, *Is this going to help me or hurt even more?* It was a chance she would have to take to mend her heart. She thought back to that day, the day she believed she'd met her soul mate.

Stephanie was at home finishing getting dressed before Robert picked her up. They were heading to the town festival. The weather was perfect. She decided to wear her comfortable jeans tonight. She wanted a casual, relaxing night. Robert walked in as she was drying her hair.

"You're not ready yet? I want to get a good seat for the fireworks," he said. Robert looked handsome in whatever he wore, and he had the personality to match.

Don't Stand Still

"I'm ready. I'm ready. Calm down. Let me just grab my shirt." Stephanie grabbed her red plaid shirt to wear over her sleeveless top. "Does this look all right to you? Stop looking in the mirror at yourself!" They both laughed.

"You look fine." He grabbed her waist and then pulled her close. "Look at us in the mirror. We are a damn good-looking couple aren't we? We should model together." He leaned down and kissed Stephanie on the forehead.

"OK, will you stop? I'm ready." Stephanie grabbed her keys. They locked up the door and turned to walk toward the event. Everything in town was in walking distance, and there were always people in the streets walking.

Stephanie enjoyed going to any of these carnivals. She wasn't sure if it was the scent of the cotton candy or the excitement of the amusement rides. She loved all the rides, and especially the Ferris wheel. Robert didn't share her love for that ride, especially when Stephanie rocked the seat at the top. It was a surprise to them that they weren't thrown off the ride each year for the commotion they caused.

What she enjoyed the most was the last night of the festival when there was a fireworks show. That was definitely her favorite part. Stephanie lay back in the grass, relaxed, and watched the sky turn different colors.

Robert and Stephanie walked through the crowd hand in hand. They played some of the games. He tried to win her a large stuffed animal, but instead won her a stuffed pencil. He was aiming for a stuffed blue parrot that Stephanie had her eye on. But when Robert handed her the stuffed pencil, she responded with a smile, "I love it."

Robert offered to get them some cotton candy. She, unable to resist, agreed it was be a good idea and waited for him at the bridge. The walking bridge looked over the festival on both sides. She watched the Ferris wheel going around and the children running into the fun house. She took a mental note that after she finished her cotton candy, she would force Robert on the Ferris wheel again. Yes, force. Robert was a well-built, confident man, but he was terrified of the Ferris wheel. Every time he agreed to go on, Stephanie promised to behave, but when they reached the top, she leaned over and rocked the car. The more nervous he got, the more she laughed. She thought it might be more difficult this year as last year had been traumatic for him. Maybe she would have to settle for going in the fun house with him. That could be fun too.

Stephanie noticed a couple below the bridge disagreeing with one another in elevated tones. There seemed to be no other spectators. She felt obligated to watch as maybe a witness to what happened—or was it the dramatic side of her that couldn't turn away? Stephanie couldn't decipher who was angry and who was upset. She thought, *Should I turn away to give them privacy?* Their emotions changed quickly. She found herself so intrigued that she didn't notice someone was standing by her side.

Stephanie turned her head, and the stranger chuckled. She took his laughter offensively and didn't know whether to walk away or say something. She decided to respond to him. "May I ask you what you're laughing at?" Stephanie's facial expression must have looked defensive, which seemed to entice him even more. She looked at him, forgetting about the couple that earlier stole her attention.

The man's look of amusement never changed as he asked, "So, do you think she had an affair on him? Do you think the argument is over money? How about jealousy? Or what if he forgot to put the toilet seat down at home?" He rattled all these possibilities off as Stephanie wondered who the guy thought he was. He seemed arrogant, but his eyes never escape Stephanie.

She responded as evenly and coolly as possible. "I'm not sure what the argument is about, but I feel it's my duty to watch over them, just in case it gets physical. I can be a witness to it. I'm not intruding. I'm trying to protect." She smiled as if she had won a fight with her older brother. She crossed her arms crossed, looking him straight in the eyes. It felt good until he responded.

"So in order to protect her, you're eavesdropping. Are you an undercover police officer? Are you a reporter? Or do you just enjoy the drama? I can tell you that I was watching because I like the drama. I don't enjoy watching people get hurt, but I do enjoy the intensity. I thrive off the sense of urgency and the adrenaline that goes through my body when a tragedy occurs. I don't like to stand still. Keep moving is my way. Like this, us speaking. I can tell you're getting angry at me, but really, why?" He paused for a moment and then reached out his hand to her. "Hello, my name is Michael Pellegrino."

Am I on candid camera? Stephanie thought. *Is this a joke that Robert put someone up to? And where is Robert? Is he watching this scenario play out? Did Robert put this man up to this?* She shook his hand and introduced herself to Michael. "Hello. Stephanie Ferrari." He was mysterious-looking. Not so tall, but dark. Handsome, definitely, but his eyes are what reeled her in. They seemed to look right through her as if he could interpret her thoughts. What was the right thing to do, stay or walk away? Stephanie looked down and noticed the couple below them had walked away, looking as if they were on the path of making up.

Stephanie and Michael sat on a bench nearby. Stephanie

wanted to sit close to the bridge to watch out for Robert. They made small talk about their jobs and what they liked to do for fun. Michael asked, "Would you ever consider sky diving or bungee jumping? Those are two things on my bucket list that I haven't had the courage to try yet."

Stephanie laughed. "I don't mean to laugh, and those ideas sound like fun, but I think that's where I draw the line. I don't think I would try them. I like to have full control, so jumping out of the sky and depending on the equipment working doesn't seem like my cup of tea. I would love to try rock climbing one day though. I don't know of a good place around here that offers it."

"I know of a place if you want to go next week." Michael said as confidently as if he were introducing his name.

Stephanie was silent for a moment. She didn't know how to respond. How could she say yes to someone she had just met.

Then Robert came back with her cotton candy in hand. She didn't quite understand his look as he stared at them. Was it anger, disappointment, or curiosity? She introduced Michael to Robert, and they shook hands. Robert sat on one side of Stephanie, and Michael on the other. Initially, it felt awkward. Stephanie tried to keep the conversation going between the three of them.

Robert stayed with them not only for the sake of her protection, but also as her "man screener." After about an hour, he asked to have a word with Stephanie.

"You two seem to have a lot in common. He's definitely cute. I'm not sure I feel comfortable leaving you alone with him though." Robert looked over at Michael. "I don't know him enough to trust him."

"We're at a festival. What can he do to me? Make me go on the Ferris wheel and shake it on the top?" She laughed, remembering those moments with Robert.

"Now that would be mean. Definitely a deal breaker!" Robert laughed along with her.

"Don't worry. I'll be fine." Stephanie continued laughing.

"But I do feel guilty that I came with you. I don't want you to leave alone. Why don't you stay with us? We can watch the fireworks together."

"Honey, don't you worry about me. I'll take a nice relaxing walk. Then I'll go home and sack out on my couch till I get your phone call to tell me how it went. I can see the fireworks from my back deck. Best part about it, I can watch them with a nice cold bottle of beer." Robert gave Stephanie a kiss on her cheek and waved good-bye to Michael.

For the rest of the afternoon, Michael and Stephanie went on a few rides with the exception of the Ferris wheel. *What is it with men and the Ferris wheel?* They spoke for hours. He worked in a restaurant, he had a large family, he was Italian, he liked making people laugh, and he liked all kinds of music except country. Michael is definitely an extrovert.

It was getting dark, which meant the fireworks would begin shortly. She didn't want to sound too aggressive in asking if he wanted to watch them together, so she tried subtlety. "I'm going to head to the field to watch the fireworks before there are no spots left."

"Sounds like you're saying good-night. Do you like watching fireworks alone? If it's your thing, I can leave you alone." Michael held out his hand to shake hers. She put her hand in his. He pulled her close and whispered in her ear, "I'm not letting you watch them alone. You're stuck with me." He turned his back with her hand still in his and walked to the field.

Stephanie couldn't understand why his whispering in her ear gave her the chills—the good kind of chills. Michael almost dragged Stephanie, and she was taken aback by his forwardness.

They found a nice spot in front of a tree. Michael sat down first, leaning against the tree, and then held his hand out for Stephanie to sit down. She wasn't sure if she should sit in front of him or beside him. She chose to sit next to him. He placed his hand on her leg as the fireworks began. It was a beautiful show.

"I'm sorry Robert missed this. I think the show was better

than last year." Stephanie said. "Not that you weren't good company."

"Nice save. I'm sure Robert saw the sky light up from his house. Ah, look there are a few more over there. Someone must be lighting them from their house." Michael stood up and held his hand out to help her to her feet.

The night soon had to come to an end. Stephanie met Michael just a few hours earlier, but she felt like she had known him for longer than that.

"Well, I should be heading home, it's getting late. It was nice meeting you, Michael." Stephanie held her hand out to him. She wasn't sure if that was the correct thing to do at this point. She wondered, *How do you say good-night; I hope to see you again?*

Michael moved her hand away and wrapped his arms around her. He gave her a bear hug and pulled back with his arms still around her. Stephanie was nervous he would try to kiss her, and she didn't want to on the first night they met. But he just looked at her, "It was nice meeting you as well, Stephanie. So what are our plans for tomorrow? How about going rock climbing with a new friend?" They made plans to get together the day after and still just stood there.

She never dreamed of going to a festival and meeting the man of her dreams. Then Michael caressed her left check and then her right and pulled her chin toward him. He looked into her eyes as he leaned down and kissed her gently. She never imagined kissing a man she had met on the same day. She would always remember her first kiss with Michael.

Days and nights passed, and their relationship grew stronger. They made plans every day to see each other the next day. The dates ranged from rock climbing, mountain biking, camping—anything fun and spontaneous. Most of the time, they didn't make plans ahead of time and, instead, planned in the moment. It was like they were meant to be. They were always on the run and never standing still. When they weren't together, they were on the phone with each other.

Don't Stand Still

Michael and Stephanie took off for weekends without a second thought. He became her everything. Stephanie felt lost when she was not by Michael's side. Stephanie was no longer Stephanie; she was now Stephanie and Michael.

They introduced one another to their families and friends. Stephanie immediately fell in love with his family. She loved spending time with his mother and sisters. It felt like she was spending time with her own family. The love between his siblings was evident when she walked through the door. Michael was affectionate toward his mom.

Stephanie's parents enjoyed Michael's company. He made them laugh and brought life to the house. Her mom advised Stephanie to take it slow. She was concerned about how fast the relationship was moving.

Robert teased Stephanie that she "lost that loving feeling" with him. He acted jealous, but she knew he was happy for her. They caught up at work about how the relationship was progressing. Robert also voiced his concern on how fast things were moving. Stephanie shrugged it off and reassured him that everything was fine. He didn't give her too hard a time about the limited time he had with her now. He understood she was happy, and he felt he had to be supportive.

A few months into their relationship, Michael packed a lunch for them and drove them to the local park. Stephanie enjoyed whatever they did each day, whether it was the movies, hiking, slow dancing at the house, or a simple picnic. While they ate lunch, Michael took her hand. "Steph, you have mustard on your face." He chuckled and wiped it off. Then he leaned over and kissed her on the nose, then her cheeks, and then her lips. He whispered, "I love you to the moon and back." It was the first time he had told her.

Stephanie reciprocated with, "I love you, more." She felt like her life was complete. She was with the man of her dreams, her soul mate.

Now that the words flowed easily, Stephanie and Michael drove down the street, and Michael would open his car window and yell out, "I love this girl!" Even though Stephanie was embarrassed with his outburst, it was a great feeling knowing how much he cared for her. But with that much love came intensity.

Michael was a great boyfriend, but he sometimes got a little controlling and jealous. It sounded silly, because they spent so much of their time together, it didn't give him much time to feel these insecurities. Stephanie overlooked all of those issues because she had fallen so deeply in love with him that nothing else mattered. Even now, thinking back, she knows all Michael ever wanted was for them to live their lives together and alone.

Their relationship was so intense due in part to the strong feelings they had for one another but also due to the spontaneity of their relationship. There was no planning, and they lived in the moment. Once Michael and Stephanie took the day off work to go to Six Flags and went on almost every ride, laughing and screaming. It was a fun-packed day. Their relationship was about fun, laughing as much as they could, and being affectionate to one another every day. It sometimes felt like they lived in their own bubble, away from the rest of the world. Michael turned to Stephanie and said, "I want you forever in my life." Stephanie felt the same way. Her response was, "Forever and always."

Michael loved to make people laugh and was constantly telling jokes. He was always the comedian in the group. Sometimes Stephanie felt overlooked and jealous. He was so busy making other people laugh, which was great, but it took his attention from her, even if it was just for that night. They were both used to giving each other 100 percent of each other's attention that it was a change to add anyone else into their "bubble" world.

When they went out with a group of friends, Michael sometimes had a few too many drinks, but Stephanie didn't mind as long as he was having fun. Everyone said how funny he was as he danced on the dance floor and called me to join him. Michael and Stephanie seemed to be the only ones dancing but neither of them cared. He sang to her regardless of all the people watching them. Stephanie took care of him if he was sick later, but now she just enjoyed what she had with him. She didn't drink as much, maybe one glass of wine to be social.

It seemed to everyone that this was a match made in heaven.

One Sunday night, Stephanie was sleeping by Michael's side. She was awakened by his touch. She opened her eyes and saw him staring at her while he caressed her face. Without speaking, he sat up and removed his shirt. He grabbed her hand and put it on his heart. He kissed each finger and then leaned down and kissed her lightly on each cheek and then her lips.

"I love you, Stephanie," he whispered. They had made love before, but this was different. He stared deeply into her eyes without speaking a word. They couldn't possibly be any closer than they were that night. Michael and Stephanie didn't have to try; they just fit like a pair of gloves. They fell asleep in each other's arms, never letting go until the morning.

***

Two months later, Michael didn't answer his cell phone,

which was strange. After a few calls went unanswered, Stephanie decided to go to his apartment. He wasn't there. She walked into his bedroom. The bed was made as if it hadn't been slept in. His closet door, slightly open, caught her eye. She opened it up, and, to her surprise, it was empty. His clothes, shoes—everything was gone.

In the living room, the albums of them were gone. They were always on the couch table, easily within reach. There was a note in their place. The note had three single words: "I'm sorry, Stephanie."

In that moment, Stephanie felt as if the apartment was on fire. Heat hit her in the face, her lungs closed up, and then her legs gave away. She lay on the floor, not knowing what was happening to her. The tears wouldn't stop. She doesn't understand.

After calling his cell phone over thirty times and leaving numerous messages, Stephanie fell asleep.

***

Don't Stand Still

Two days went by. Michael never came home. Stephanie's life stopped for those two days. She sat there, hoping for the phone to ring or hoping for him to walk through the door. She paced around the apartment, talking to herself about the last few weeks of their relationship.

She wondered if it was something she said or did? *Did he mention that he had to go away, and he was just sorry he didn't have time to say good-bye? How can I find him? How can I get him back?* She felt like she was losing control.

Stephanie refused to answer her phone. She missed calls from her sisters, Robert and her mom. She wanted to be left alone. She didn't know what to tell anyone. She was hoping it was just a misunderstanding or a bad nightmare that she would soon wake from. She was not ready to see anyone but Michael.

She heard a noise at the door. Her heart raced, and she jumped up from the floor and ran to the door. "Michael, Michael is that you?"

Don't Stand Still

It was Robert, showing up at Michael's house to find her.

"No!" She cried as she hit him in the chest with her fists. "No! It's not you. Why?" She punched Robert's chest till she had nothing else to give. She was emotionally, physically and mentally drained.

They both sat on the floor. Robert didn't say a word. He just held her tightly, rocking back and forth with her.

The mix of feelings was overwhelming. She was angry that it was Robert at the door and not Michael; she was relieved that he was there to help her understand why her life is now changing.

"Why? Why did he leave? What did I do? I love him. I feel like I can't breathe without him. Please, help fix this." Stephanie was crying in Robert's arms. "Please. I can't live without him. Help me fix this. What can we do? Do you think he's OK?" She was terrified that she would never see Michael again.

Robert pulled Stephanie closer. He rubbed her back as she let out all her emotions. "I don't understand why he would want to leave you. We'll make it through this. I'll help you, I promise." He wiped her tears away. "I know you're hurting now. There are no answers that anyone can give you that will make this any better. I love you, honey. I'll stay here with you as long as you need me to." Robert sat there as tears escaped his eyes. He felt her pain.

What could have possibly gone wrong? Stephanie thought.

She didn't understand to this day. Yes, at the time, she mentioned marriage and children to him. They dated for almost a year, and it seemed like a natural conversation at that time. He never came out and said, "No." He just smiled and then either started wrestling with her or carried her to the bedroom. Stephanie didn't think anything of any of this till now. *Could those talks be what pushed him away?*

That is the short version of the story of Michael and Stephanie.

Don't Stand Still

Tonight was not about finding someone.

It was more about letting loose and having fun.

—Stephanie

Chapter 5

Jumping In

It was around three o'clock in the afternoon. Robert and Stephanie were still on the beach, watching the waves. It was nice to relive her past and talk about the good times without guilt over feeling alive about it and then feeling truly sad and angry about the ending.

"Thank you for letting me do this today. I know it's hard on you, too. You took really good care of me. I'm grateful for your support, guidance, and friendship. Everything you've done for me helped me during the worst time of my life. My family appreciates it too. You're my knight in shining armor." Stephanie leaned over and kissed him on the cheek.

Robert was such a great friend. During the whole breakup,

Don't Stand Still

Stephanie's nerves were shot. All she did was cry and sleep. She didn't want to socialize with anyone. She wouldn't go out or answer the phone. She wanted to be alone in every way. Then one afternoon, the inevitable happened, and, because they lived in a small town, it ran like rapid fire. Everyone seemed to know that "Stephanie Ferrari took a nervous breakdown." As much as Robert wanted to protect her from all the rumors, she heard them. The rumors bothered her, but they also made her stronger. Some people have to hit rock bottom before they regain their strength.

Stephanie knew she would never have a love like that again, but did she really want to? To have as much intensity as they did was not healthy. No relationship has that much greatness all the time. Stephanie felt terrific when she and Michael were together, but when they were apart, she felt as if she couldn't breathe and couldn't live without him by her side.

She was starting to become her own person again. Her career, as a publisher, was moving along, she was catching up with her family, and now she was preparing to go out for the night with friends.

The morning's talk with Robert seemed to give Stephanie a clear perspective on her future. She deserved to be happy again. She wanted to be happy again. It might be hard to take that first step in living, but who better to start it with than her best friend, Robert. Stephanie nudged his arm, "Let's get back home so we can get dressed for dinner. Let's get this party started." And they both laughed heading back to her house.

Stephanie jumped in the shower with a mimosa waiting for her on the counter. "I'm going to be a while. I want to shave my legs," she yelled out to Robert. She chuckled in the shower, knowing he'd have a smart comment to that.

Robert responded, "I guess you're planning to have a good night tonight!"

Stephanie and Robert were both dressed to impress and, coincidently, had color-coordinated their outfits.

Carla was running late, so they amended their plans.

Don't Stand Still

Stephanie believed it was because Carla didn't want to drive them in case they backed out on the full night of events. They took a few pictures out on the deck before they headed out to meet Carla. Stephanie's photo albums at home were now of her family and of her and Robert.

They had dinner at a small restaurant in the city. Stephanie had chicken alfredo with pasta. She also enjoyed not one, but two, glasses of wine. The food wasn't great, but a band played outside. Stephanie felt relaxed, and she decided this would be her last drink. *What are the odds of talking Carla into staying here and not going to the club?* Stephanie thought. They danced outside for most of the night, with the cool breeze hitting them. It seemed to be perfect. She wasn't sweating and no one nudged her or pushed through the crowd like they did at the clubs. She became angry when the sweat of a stranger's body hit her. She didn't want to be angry tonight. And even Carla seemed happy staying where they were.

The three of them danced together for most of the night.

Don't Stand Still

When they danced, Robert and Stephanie were more in sync than Robert and Carla were. But Robert kept up with both of the women. He looked like a lucky man on the dance floor as he twirled them around. It turned out to be a fun night for all of them. Stephanie was grateful for accepting the invitation to go out.

There was an hour till closing. The band announced they would come back next month. Stephanie mentioned to Robert that she would like to come back to see them.

Carla looked like she was getting tired. She sat at the table watching Robert and Stephanie dancing. They looked like a happy couple dancing the night away. Robert was a great dancer, especially after he had a few drinks. He kept lifting Stephanie up swinging her around. Stephanie hadn't laughed that hard in so long.

She looked over at a group of people who passed them. Someone looked over at her as he walked away. For some reason, she couldn't stop looking. Their eyes met and followed each other. She wasn't sure if she was looking to figure out what he was looking at, or if she was actually interested in looking at him.

Robert was oblivious to what was going on. He was crowd-watching himself. As Stephanie looked back at Robert to point the person out to him, he was gone. Stephanie thought, *Oh well, I was imagining it.* Then she laughed and thought, *Maybe he was checking Robert out.*

Robert and Stephanie continued to dance until he was tapped on his shoulder. He turned around to look at the tapper and then back at Stephanie. It was by the same man she had been looking at, asking if he could cut in. Robert agreed and walked away to sit with Carla. Stephanie could just imagine what their conversation was like.

There was no discussion for Stephanie and this unknown man, because they were dancing in front of the speakers. They smiled at one another while they danced for three or four songs. As they danced, she went over a checklist in her head: he can dance, he's cute, and he's a nice dresser. And he had the courage to cut in on her and Robert.

Don't Stand Still

The most interesting thing about him was that while they were dancing, he just stared into her eyes. It was weird. They didn't speak, but they almost seemed like they did through their dancing. It was actually fun for Stephanie to dance with someone other than Robert. She loved Robert, but it was nice to know someone else wanted to dance with her because he was interested in her. Stephanie's goal was to have a good time, but she had no intention of meeting anyone.

It was getting late, and the restaurant was closing. The band was packing up to leave. Stephanie and her new friend stood off to the side, away from the table where Robert and Carla were sitting. They finally introduced themselves.

"Hi. I'm Curt." He shook her hand. "It was nice dancing with you tonight. Do you come here often?" And he smiled.

"Hi. Stephanie. You're a good dancer. I haven't been out like this in a long time. The band was great tonight. I came here with my friends Robert and Carla." They seem to be waiting for me over there." Stephanie pointed over to them. She didn't want to tell him she had been a hermit for almost a year. Instead she mentioned her friends waiting to insinuate she would be leaving with them, in case he had any other thoughts. She had been out of the field for a while, so she wasn't sure what men thought of someone they just met. She felt bad for her friends waiting for her. She walked toward them.

"Yeah, my friends are waiting for me too, but they're outside. Here's my business card. I'll write my cell phone number on the back. You'll have a few different ways to get in touch with me if you'd like to. You have my work number, cell, and e-mail address. I hope you'll call."

They stood there for a moment, looking at one another, and then he reached over and hugged her good-bye. Stephanie yelled, "Good night," to him as he walked out the door.

Stephanie put his business card in her back pocket and then walked over to her friends. She was still wide awake from all the dancing. But poor Carla looked exhausted. Stephanie felt bad that Carla had wanted to have the night on the town, but she was now the exhausted one of the bunch. They decided to take her home first. Stephanie sincerely thanked Carla for not giving up on her. She was really glad she pushed her to go out. They hadn't laughed that hard together in a long time. It was a good night overall.

Stephanie was surprised she didn't get many questions about Curt. She didn't have much to offer anyway, except that he was a good dancer. She informed them about him giving her his contact information. She commented, "It's only a number, I doubt I'll even call it. Tonight was not about finding someone. It was more about letting loose and having fun."

It was a good day, all in all. Stephanie caught up on cleaning, went for a run, made an emotional breakthrough, and then went out and had a great time. Carla and Robert even seemed to bond. They had many laughs, and Stephanie ended it with someone's business card, though, she wasn't sure would call the number on it.

Don't Stand Still

Robert, I would marry you tomorrow! Don't tease me.

—Stephanie

Chapter 6

Moving Forward

Today was Sunday. The weather forecaster seemed to get the weather right so far today; there wasn't a cloud in the sky. Stephanie wanted to spend as much time as she could outside. The sun was just right. It was a perfect day for a hike or to read a book on the back deck.

Unfortunately, Robert had a family commitment, so Stephanie had the day to herself. She sat on her deck, reading one of her Nicholas Sparks books. She could read his books over and over and still cry out loud at the end. She was glad one of her close friends, Michelle, let her borrow one of his first books, *A Walk to Remember*. Since then Stephanie has read and collected all of his books.

Don't Stand Still

She had no plans for the rest of the day except to relax. What more could she ask for? The beep from the oven let her know it was preheated. She put some chocolate chip cookies in the oven, first stealing a taste of the cookie dough.

She noticed one more load of laundry to put in the washer. Laundry was one of those chores that took her a long time to finish. She sometimes left the clothes in the washer or dryer for too long. But what took her the longest was actually putting the clothes away after she folded them. She often folded them and left them in the basket. While she was taking her last load to the laundry room, she noticed something white sticking out of her pants pocket. It was the business card from the night before. She put it on the counter and then brought her laundry downstairs. When Stephanie came back up, she took the card and the cordless phone outside. *Do I or don't I?* she thought. *What do I have to lose, right?*

Since it was Sunday, Stephanie couldn't call his work number. *Should I call his work number and then just leave a message to have him call me back?* But she despised when people played those types of games. She only had thirteen minutes before she had to take the cookies out of the oven. She dialed his cell phone number. After the first ring, she got nervous. What would she say if and when he picked up? She didn't know anything about him except that she danced with him for a few songs. After the second ring, she wondered if she was ready for this. Before she could change her mind, Curt picked up.

Stephanie didn't want to say hello back. She wasn't ready, but she couldn't hang up. What if he had caller ID, and she hung up? Her stomach made flips. After a few seconds, she spoke up. "Hello Curt. This is Stephanie." Maybe if she stayed quiet, he'd do the rest of the talking. Then she thought. *Maybe he doesn't even remember me.*

"Hi, Stephanie. I'm glad you called. I realized on the ride home that I didn't get your number. I started to feel like you had all the control." Curt laughed. "So, what are you doing on this warm, sunny day?"

"I'm taking some cookies out of the oven in a few minutes.

Then I'm just going to relax on the deck, reading a book." This seemed easier than she thought. *Just go with the flow, as if you're speaking to Robert.* Stephanie let out a sigh of relief that it was not awkward yet. That had to be a good sign. It wasn't like she would marry him. They were just having a conversation on the phone.

"Relaxing, reading a book, and eating cookies. Hopefully they're chocolate chip. Nothing beats a nice warm chocolate-chip cookie. I'm just home watching some TV and thinking how much I loathe Mondays." Curt laughed. "I'm OK when Monday hits and I get into the groove of things. It's the anticipation of going back to work after a nice weekend. I manage well though, probably because I actually like my work." He paused, "What do you do?"

Stephanie put Curt on hold to take the cookies out of the oven. Then they talked for almost an hour about what their work, the colleges they went to, and what they did for fun. He enjoyed reading, sports, and outdoor activities. One of his recent adventures was skydiving. It was like she was talking to a long-lost friend. It felt comfortable, and Stephanie wasn't nervous any longer.

Don't Stand Still

They laughed about how Stephanie made dessert before she started thinking about what she was making for dinner. "My priorities are straight. Eat the comfort food before the main dish," Stephanie said.

Curt started the conversation about the night before, "Last night was alright. I mean, I followed my friends around for most of the night till I noticed you. I got a break from taking care of a friend of mine who had too much to drink."

"So that's what I was, a break from the drama." Stephanie laughed.

Curt laughed along. "No, I don't mean it like that. I'm glad we met. It was the best part of the night. I'm sorry I cut in while you were dancing with that other man."

"Oh yeah, Robert, the other man. He's my best friend, the one man in my life. I had fun too. I'm glad I decided to go out." Stephanie then became silent, waiting for him to speak.

The next thing she did surprised her, but didn't seem to

surprise Curt at all. "Would you like to come over for dinner? I can microwave the chocolate chip cookies." They both laughed.

"Under one condition." Curt responded

"Oh no, what's that stipulation?" Stephanie laughed.

Curt hesitated, "As long as you don't have to cook. Let's make this night simple. We can order take-out."

She didn't know whether to take offense to his objection to her cooking or think of it as a neutral dinner arrangement. They agreed on a time, and then Stephanie gave him her address.

After she hung up, she cleaned up. Not much was needed since she did a detailed cleaning a few days ago. When the house was done, it was time to get dressed for the date. Was it a date, or was it two people getting together?

They were staying in, so she didn't want to get dressed up too fancy. She put on a nice pair of capris and a sleeveless shirt. The final to-do item was to call Robert. She dialed his number as she walked around lighting all her candles. "Hey Robert, are you home yet? How was the cookout?"

"It was great. They actually had a clam boil too. My parents say hello. They wanted to know why you chose to sit home alone rather than coming over here." Robert chuckled, "They were joking, insinuating that they took it offensively. I explained that girls need their alone time. They never give up hoping we'll get married. Maybe we should just do it. What do you think? Stephanie, my love, will you marry me?" Robert laughed. "So what did you do today besides clean?"

Stephanie responded, "Robert, I would marry you tomorrow! Don't tease me." They both laughed "I called Curt from the other night. Remember him? I asked him to come over for dinner. Sounds crazy huh? We spoke for almost an hour on the phone. It was comfortable. The conversation just flowed. I mentioned you're the only man in my life. It didn't scare him away though. Anyway, I wanted to call you to tell you so that if I don't answer, you'll know it's because I have company." She anxiously waited for his response. If Robert disagreed with what she was doing, she would rescind the invitation. She took his opinion seriously now more than ever.

"Well good for you. You have fun. Call me when he leaves—if he leaves." Robert laughed. "Seriously, think of it as meeting a new friend. Nothing says he has to be your soul mate or lover. He can simply be a new friend. Wait, maybe lover wouldn't hurt either. Everyone needs a little loving. God knows I do." Robert had to stop speaking he was laughing so much.

"You know he won't be spending the night here. It's the first time we've seeing each other, not counting a few dances the other night. And there was only one soul mate for me." Stephanie was a little defensive, even though she knew he was joking. "My love isn't good enough for you? You're the only one sharing my bed for the last year or so. I'm satisfied with our arrangements. I'll talk to you later. Love you." As they said their good-byes, Stephanie wondered if Curt understood he would be leaving tonight. She didn't even know him, but she invited him over. Stephanie started doubting herself. Maybe she should have met him at a restaurant, not at her house.

Don't Stand Still

Well, then, I guess the pressure is on for me to prove I'm

more exciting than a book.

—Curt

Chapter 7

Beginning Again

Curt arrived with a bouquet of wildflowers in one hand. The other held at least ten menus for them to choose from for dinner. He sorted the menus by food type: Chinese, pizza, Italian, and subs. Stephanie was impressed with the preparation of menus but more impressed with the flower arrangement.

"Thank you very much for the flowers. They're my favorites. I'm not a rose type of person. They're too expensive. I love yellow and purple flowers," Stephanie said as he walked in the front door. "Come in, I'm glad you found the house OK."

She handed him a bottle of Samuel Adams Summerfest beer and picked up her glass of wine that was on the counter. They discussed what their preferred beverages were earlier in the day.

She had to be prepared as well.

"Thanks for the drink. My car told me the directions all the way here—just like having a passenger-seat driver, except it wasn't annoying." They both laughed. "I brought some menus I printed online of local restaurants. Do you have any preference? I'm up for anything." Curt dropped the menus on the kitchen table.

"If you don't have a preference, I have an idea." Stephanie smiled and flipped all the menus face down and mixed them around. "Turn around with your back toward the table, and reach over and grab one."

Curt did so. "Aren't you adventurous? O, drum roll please…We'll be having Chinese food for dinner. Good choice. That's what I was going to choose."

They ordered the food, a little bit of everything, and then went together for the ride to pick up the food. She was pleasantly surprised when he opened her door. After she pleaded with him, he agreed that she could pay for the food under the condition that he would pay for the next time. Stephanie thought, *Hmm, he's planning a next time. We will see how this night goes.*

Stephanie suggested they eat outside on the deck, and Curt agreed. She had never taken over an hour to eat dinner, but they seemed to talk about everything.

Curt came from a small family. He was close with his younger sister, Lana. He took her to the zoo, aquarium, and circus. She wanted to be a marine biologist when she got older. He told her he'd help her reach her dreams in any way he could. It was nice to hear him speaking about his family, which seemed like close and loving.

Stephanie figured she would clean up from dinner, but as she stood up, she was surprised to see Curt do so as well. She brought in the dirty dishes as he brought in the leftover food containers. She wasn't used to someone helping her clean up. She thought about Michael. He wouldn't think about cleaning up, but that was fine for her because she enjoyed taking care of him. She thought *I cannot compare the two of them tonight.*

Don't Stand Still

"Where do you keep your Tupperware containers?" Curt asked. He looked at her as if he knew he was bringing her back to today. "Sorry, you seemed like you were in deep thought. I can put the leftovers away if you want."

Stephanie handed him a few containers. "I'm just not used to people helping me clean up. I usually take care of the mess. You took me off guard, that's all." She really looked at him for the first time tonight.

Curt wore blue jeans with a fitted gray short-sleeved shirt that showed the definition in his arms. She was happy with what she saw. He seemed calm and responsible, he liked to talk, and he was respectful to her. She reminded herself that this was just two people hanging out and not a date.

Curt smiled. "I don't think you were the only one eating all this food, and I'm not used to anyone cleaning up after me. I promise, you won't have to clean up my mess ever." He placed the containers in the fridge, took out another Sam Adams, and poured her another glass of wine.

Don't Stand Still

Stephanie heard the word *ever*, and, for the first time, she felt nervous. She hadn't heard that word in a long time. She had *forever* before, but that didn't last. This would be a hard step, but she would be open-minded. This was a breakthrough for her.

After they were done with the straightening up, they grabbed their refills and went back outside. They stood up, looking over the railing. Curt put down his drink and held Stephanie in front of him.

She leaned her head against his chest and looked out into the ocean. "It's such a nice night out. I love listening to the waves and looking out at the water. The sight of the ocean and the sound of the waves—they're my chocolate."

It felt awkward showing attention to someone she didn't know well. Is this how relationships began? He held her the way Michael held her. Stephanie thought, *Is this the right thing to do?* Even though Curt seemed like a nice guy, she felt like a part of her still belonged to Michael. She wasn't sure she was willing to let that go, at least not yet.

Don't Stand Still

Curt was quiet, rubbing her arms and holding her close. "Are you sure you're not getting cold? We can go inside."

Stephanie struggled to not look up at him, but he turned her to look at him. She tried not to make eye contact for the fear of what would happen next.

She looked up at him, ready to respond. Curt looked into her eyes without speaking. He held her face with a hand on each cheek and leaned down to kiss her. It was a soft, short kiss—not passionate but sweet. She leaned in against his chest and stood in his arms for a few minutes.

Stephanie felt as though she were in a trance. She held his hand to walk him back into the house. "Let's warm up inside. We can play one hundred questions to get to know one another more." They both laughed to break the tension.

For the next hour, they spoke about their longest relationships, dislikes, weaknesses, and strengths. Curt's longest relationship was a little over three years. They broke up when he caught her with another man. There was hurt in his eyes as he spoke about his ex-girlfriend.

Stephanie was surprised how easily she opened up about Michael. Opening up about him wasn't so much the struggle. It was hearing other people judge his actions. She still got upset if anyone put him down or said anything negative about him.

Curt didn't go down that road. He just listened. He eventually made only one comment, "Your first love."

Stephanie thought, *My only love.*

She went to the kitchen for the plate of cookies. She sat down beside him, and he went into the kitchen. Stephanie turned to watch him. Curt opened a few cabinets to find glasses and poured them both a glass of milk. He then grabbed some napkins and came back to the couch.

"What's good on TV tonight or do you want to rent a movie?" he asked as he dipped a cookie in his milk.

Stephanie was amazed at how comfortable he was in her

house and was surprised it didn't bother her.

She smiled, looking at the milk on his top lip. "Are you sure it's not too late to start a movie? We have work in the morning. I don't mind; I'm a night owl. If you leave, I'll just read. You have some milk on your top lip, mister." They both laughed till he leaned over and kissed her to share the milk.

"Well, then, I guess the pressure is on for me to prove I'm more exciting than a book. Let's watch a movie." Curt picked up the remote and selected a comedy from On Demand. She had all the movie channels, so there was no charge for the On Demand premium channels.

Stephanie leaned back against his chest. They cuddled up on the couch, laughing and watching the movie, *The Proposal* with Sandra Bullock. Stephanie looked up at him to make a comment but kissed him instead. This time the kiss was more passionate and meaningful. She wasn't sure whether it was the comfort or the attraction between them, but she felt this could be the beginning of something good.

Don't Stand Still

And it was.

Part Two

The Future

Stephanie, will you stay with me forever as my best friend

and my wife?

—Curt

Chapter 8

Closing In

Friday was the best day of the workweek. The energy during the day was contagious. The start of the weekend, payday, and dress-down day. Stephanie enjoyed walking through the city, especially on Fridays. It seemed as if everyone were either out walking or driving by—the spirit of the city. This afternoon, she was meeting Curt for lunch for their usual fish-and-chips ritual. Stephanie thought, *I can't believe it's been almost two years for Curt and me.*

Time went by so fast since their first date. They became best friends, lovers, and each other's "always" in this time frame. They saw each other at least three times a week for the first year. After that, they basically lived with one another.

Don't Stand Still

Stephanie created a tradition of getting together with Robert and Carla once a month for dinner. She enjoyed this time with her friends to catch up about Curt, work, and family. She thanked Carla numerous of times for forcing her to go out that night. Robert and Stephanie got together more often, sometimes with Curt and sometimes alone. Their sleepovers diminished to none. She spent quality time with him but not in that way. She had a stable, healthy relationship with her friends and Curt.

Curt proposed on Valentine's Day. It was such a special night. They went to an Italian restaurant for dinner and then a walk in the city. They stood on a bridge looking over the water. When Stephanie turned around to tell him she was cold, he was on one knee. Suddenly, she wasn't cold any longer.

"Stephanie, will you stay with me forever as my best friend and my wife?"

Tears of happiness filled her eyes. "Yes!"

Curt picked her up and swung her around. They were both

very happy. That night, they visited both sets of parents to announce their news. Their faces hurt from smiling so much. Then Stephanie called Robert on speaker phone to ask him to be the best man at their wedding.

Of course, Robert said, "Yes." He was as excited as she was. He said he couldn't wait to see her and help plan the wedding.

Since then, both Stephanie and Curt had been in planning mode as much as they could be with their busy careers. After a few weeks, they decided they didn't want a long engagement.

Everything seemed to fall into place. They loved each other and didn't want to wait too long to be husband and wife. Stephanie couldn't be happier.

Even though it was Friday, it was been a busy day in the office. Stephanie had four hours to catch up on work before her lunch date with Curt. She worked through her morning to-do list. She also had another list for when she returned to the office. The lists consisted of work and personal tasks. Work action items came first since they were deadline-driven. She had four articles to write and forward for approvals and had to start next week's reviews. She loved her job, but, most of all, she was proud of where she was from where she began as a receptionist. There had been many hurdles to cross, but with the support of her family and Robert, she made it. Life was good. Perfect.

Robert walked over in his dazzling blue suit with a hot chocolate and muffin in hand. "Good morning, my sweetheart. I brought you breakfast. I doubt you've had anything to eat yet. And you know I'm always right." He kissed her on the cheek.

As he handed her the corn muffin, Stephanie thought, *Wow am I becoming predictable.* Always the same breakfast every morning. She didn't think she even tasted it. She thought, *Take time to enjoy your food.* But then she reminded herself of all the work she had to get done before she met Curt.

"Good Morning, Robert. How was your night? Tell me you did something exciting. Did you meet anyone? What time did you get home anyway? I called you around eleven, and you didn't answer." Thursday nights in the city were like Friday nights in the city. People were everywhere in the streets, bars, and cafés.

Robert went out every Thursday night. Stephanie loved hearing his stories on Friday mornings. It was like she was living vicariously through him. As he told her about his adventure about meeting another Mr. Right, her phone rang. "Oh no. I want to hear the rest. Don't leave." She answered the phone.

It was Mary, the receptionist. "I have someone on the phone for you. I think it's your brother. Can you please give him your direct extension next time?"

Stephanie thought, *When I was the receptionist, I never gave anyone attitude. I just transferred the call.* Mary complained all the time when the call comes through the main number. It usually was Stephanie's brother, whom she consistently gave her direct number. He could have even called her cell. She honestly thought he did it to just to irritate Mary.

"Can you tell him I'll call him back in a few minutes? I'm

finishing up a conversation with my manager."

Before she disconnected, Stephanie heard Mary whisper, "I am not your secretary."

She really needed to go buy Mary flowers, candy, or something to smooth this over. But her priorities were straight. She needed to hear the rest of Robert's story. Then she would call her brother back. "Go on. Did you give him your number or take his? You should have given him yours. Did you two go out after the club for breakfast? How did you leave it? What does he look like?"

Robert described his new friend in detail—tall, blond hair, and on the thinner side. Robert had his share of bad relationships but had come a long way in choosing the right people, even to just be friends with. "We're going to dinner on Saturday night. He called me this morning just to say good morning. Isn't that the sweetest? You need to meet him. Do you think you and Curt can come along on Saturday? I told him all about you."

Marcia, the office manager, walked toward them, and

Don't Stand Still

Robert and Stephanie said their good-byes for now.

"You're going to lunch with Curt today, right?" Robert asked. "I'm running to the bank across the street. Do you want me to do anything for you while I'm there?" As always, Robert read her mind.

"It's our Friday ritual. Curt and I are going for fish and chips. If you don't mind, yes. Can you deposit this money for me?" Stephanie gave him her deposit slip with the checks and cash to go with it. She didn't know what she would do without him. "Thank you. I owe you one. Actually I owe you more than one!"

The phone rang again. As Stephanie yelled bye to Robert, she picked up the phone. She responded as cheerily as she could.

Mary didn't even ask if Stephanie could take the call this time. She just transferred him to her line.

Stephanie says in her most frustrated voice, "Vin, why do you do that to her? You know she hates when you call the main line. It's not like you don't know my direct extension. Come on!"

She felt like hanging up on him out of frustration, but she didn't, in case it was an emergency.

Then Stephanie's stomach dropped and she sat back in her chair, when the male voice on the phone said, "I don't have your direct extension, but if you want to give it to me, I'll hang up and call you back."

She remained speechless. The muffin was not sitting well in her stomach.

"Steph, how have you been? I hope it's alright that I called you. Are you there?" His voice had always been so confident, as if he could take on the world, but this call was different. He sounded uneasy and shaky, as if he was nervous.

Stephanie didn't know what the right decision was, whether to hang up on him or listen to what he had to say. She finally had the nerve to speak up. "Are you OK? Why are you calling me? Is something wrong?" She never imagined those would be her first words to the man who broke her heart years ago. She completely ignored the question of how she was doing. Stephanie couldn't put into words how she was doing right then. She didn't think she could answer that question honestly. The emotions that flowed through her ranged from anger, happiness, sadness, and confusion. Could he need money? Was his family alright, or was he not OK? As she waited for his response, she speculated about all the possibilities. Why was she so concerned with how Michael was doing?

"Stephanie, everything's fine. You probably want to hang up on me, don't you? I know it's a surprise to hear from me. I've dialed your number a few times in the last few months but was too afraid to actually go through with it." The only time he called her Stephanie, besides when they first met, was their infamous breakup.

It was nine o'clock, and a rush of anxiety and adrenaline went through her, something she hadn't felt in a few years. Life had been so relaxed, predictable, healthy, and good.

"Would it be crazy of me to think we could meet for lunch

today? I'd really like to see you. I need to talk to you about us, about what happened. I have some things to explain to you. I know I don't deserve the chance, but, please, Steph. Please. I promise I won't take much of your time." Michael stopped speaking. waiting for Stephanie's response.

The anger set in. Stephanie believed she could do this without raising her voice so that the whole office didn't hear. "So, you're OK? You're not hurt. Everyone in your family is OK. But you want me to come meet you for lunch to talk about us. There are no us. 'Us' stopped years ago when you disappeared. I can't just get up and go with you. I'm meeting my fiancé, Curt, today. It's great that now you're ready to talk about us. It's been over three years since we broke up. I called you for months asking you—no, wait—begging you to talk to me. All I heard was your voice mail. Tell me one reason why I shouldn't replicate that response to you. You bastard." Her face felt like it was burning up. She was so angry that tears accumulated in her eyes. *Who does he think he is that he can attempt to turn my world around with this one phone call*? Stephanie looked around to see if anyone heard her and then walked over to her door.

"Dennis, if anyone is looking for me, I'm on a conference call right now." She told her coworker. She then directed her attention back to her call. "If you have anything to say, I'll give you the time right now on the phone. Why? Because I'm a better person than you are." As she said it, she was nervous. What could he want to tell her, and was she ready to hear it? She also felt guilty that a small part of her was happy to hear from him, if for no other reason that she would finally know why he left that day.

One of her first reactions was to instant message Robert to tell him who she was on the phone with, but she knew he would come in and disconnect the call. She kept this conversation to herself for now.

Michael began speaking in a low tone, "Steph, I miss you. Please, before you interrupt, yell, or curse at me, let me say what I need to say. I understand that you probably hate me right now. Who am I to ask for the chance to speak to you when I didn't give you a chance? Who am I to think you will be there for me when I wasn't there for you? I know I don't deserve you or your time." He stopped, not sure if he was waiting for Stephanie to respond or not, but she remained quiet, interested in what he needed to say to her after all this time.

Michael started again. "I was completely wrong for just ending our relationship so abruptly. I didn't know how else to respond at the time. You were ready for marriage, children, and a future. Back then, I wasn't at the same place as you. I liked what we had: spontaneity. We had fun just being us. I wanted to travel and continue the exciting carefree life we shared. I felt it wasn't possible to have it all. I know I was wrong in feeling that way. It was selfish. I've regretted it every day of my life since. I want you to know that I was hurting being away from you, but I understand your hurt must have been multiplied since I didn't leave an explanation. And for that, I'm sorry. If I could turn back time, I would have changed my actions into words." His voice cracked.

It was the tone that always brought Stephanie back to him.

Don't Stand Still

The image of him sitting there on the phone, upset, hurt her. She always wanted to be there for him to protect him from pain. But she needed to be strong for her relationship with Curt. She loved Curt more than anything. He was the best thing that had ever happened to her.

It was OK for Stephanie to be there for Michael. It wasn't like she was running into his arms. She was just listening to him.

The phone lines were quiet at either end. Stephanie didn't know whether he needed to say more, but she took the opening to speak up. "Now you let me speak, I'm sorry that you're upset. Yes, we had a great relationship. I was extremely happy with you. I was so much in love with you and our relationship. It was always intense and exciting, but after you left me with no indication why, I lost it. I don't think you can understand how badly that hurt me. When a large portion of you disappears, you're lost. I didn't know who I was without you. I went from being very upset to angry. It took me a while, with lots of support from my family and friends, to move on. Eventually I decided to let go. Since then, I grew up.

We're adults now. I have my life, and you have yours. I'm not going to say to you that I didn't cry when you decided it was over. It hurt every day for me, all day. There were months I felt like I couldn't breathe without you. I replayed our whole relationship over and over in my head to try to figure out what I did wrong. But then I met Curt. My life has been so different since then." That was not a lie. It was different. Different could mean many things: safe, happy, calm, and secure.

Michael's response was a mixture of surprise and anger at the same time. It sounded as if he couldn't believe Stephanie was rejecting him. This was not the normal scenario. In the past, he would call her back after minor fights, and then Stephanie would be back in his arms once again. All she needed was to hear the tears, and she would stop what she was doing to start her life back up with him.

This time was different—different for her, and different for them. Stephanie had built a life of her own that she was satisfied with. She was planning a wedding with a wonderful man who loved her. Curt would never intentionally hurt her.

"Stephanie, no one will ever love you the way that I loved you. We were each other's first loves. Yes, I know about Curt. My family kept me up-to-date on your relationship. This thing, this relationship with Curt is 'safe,' but not as exciting as ours ever was. Does he look at you in the eyes as I did? Does he touch your face before he kisses you as I did? Does he yell out in the streets to people that he loves you as I did? What we had was unique and cannot be replaced. I'm telling you I still love you. I'm telling you that I know I can't live without you. Please, Steph, just give me another chance. All I want you to do is see me once. Look me in the eyes, and tell me you don't love me. Tell me that there's no spark as we look at each other. No matter how mad we were at each other, once we looked in each other's eyes, nothing else mattered. If you meet with me today, I promise I'll leave you alone if that's what you want. Steph, don't you think it's worth one last chance to see each other, even if it is to say good-bye? We were once soul mates. Don't you think we owe this to one another?"

Don't Stand Still

Michael pleaded. He has always been confident but today he is desperate, and it was just for her.

It seemed like hours went by as Stephanie contemplated how to respond. Did she even know how she wanted to respond or what she should say? Stephanie was shaking now. The tears were no longer prisoners in her eyes; they were able to escape. She knew what she needed to say, and the need had to override her want. It would definitely hurt, but the words needed to be spoken.

"Michael, I will always have a place for you in my heart. I will never forget all the crazy things we did together. We had a great past with some ups and downs. I promise you, I'll remember the ups and pack away those downs. Yes, no relationship will ever compare to what we had. I understand that as much as you. I never intended to replace our relationship. I loved you with every ounce of myself. My life started again after a long time of being depressed and lost. I'm happy now. I'm actually getting married in a few months, but I guess you already knew that. I'm sorry, Michael. You know I hate to hear you upset." It was true.

Don't Stand Still

Stephanie was hurting for him now. Hearing him upset was killing her inside. She knew she couldn't be on the phone any longer. Michael wasn't responding to her with words.

Stephanie watched the hands of the clock turn. It was almost nine thirty. "I have to go. I have a meeting that starts in an hour. I want you to be happy. I'm confident you'll have your happiness. You'll meet someone who is perfect for you. I will always care about you." Again, she waited for his response, not sure if she was waiting for him to disagree with what she said or hang up on her.

Finally, he spoke as she was about to say good-bye. "I'm not going to say I'll let you go, because that would be untrue. I've never let you go. You've remained in my heart from the first day I met you. I'll never stop loving you, and I'm not going to give up on you. You are my angel. Good-bye."

The dial tone that followed seemed louder than Stephanie had ever heard it.

Don't Stand Still

After looking at her phone for a few minutes, she walked over to her door. She opened it and then stared out on to the floor. Everyone was on their phones or typing on their computers. The liveliness of the office was as intense as it could be that early in the morning. The schedule seemed to be consistent day in and day out—something her life had never been when she was with Michael. She walked back into her office and sat down in front of her computer.

Stephanie had been prepared for her meeting since last night. It was one of those scheduled things she did every night before she left work. She printed the calendar along with each meeting request to note any comments.

Now she sat there with her thoughts roaming in her head. *Would it have hurt if I met him just for a coffee?* she thought. *Is it right that I'm letting him hurt as he hurt me? Maybe I should have been the bigger person.* It didn't matter now. She hung up the phone, and she ended the conversation. She probably wouldn't see or hear from Michael again. If there had been a chance to talk, that time was over.

The phone seemed like it was reaching out to her. She felt lost in her own office. *Need to move on; live with no regrets*, she thought. In her head, she recited all the advice she received from her counselor. Who should she call? Stephanie almost called Curt to tell him about her morning surprise, but then she decided not to. She'd tell him at lunch. It would give them something exciting to talk about—not that the wedding discussions were not exciting. Stephanie was not yet ready to talk to Robert about it either. He would have too many questions that she didn't have the answers to. She stared at the phone, thinking back to the conversation. She thought her response was right. Of course it was right. Could she be dreaming, or could this be a prank? Was it really him after all this time? Did she respond in the correct way? Michael did seem really sorry for what he put her through. He sounded different on the phone. He had always held the cards in their relationship.

This Michael was really upset and hurt. Stephanie was always there to take care of him when he was sick or had too much to drink. She wondered who would be there for him now.

Stephanie started doubting herself. She thought she maybe should have met him one day. Of course, she would pick the date and time. Maybe Michael deserved to see for himself that their eyes don't meet like they did in the past. Not only did Stephanie's eyes belong to Curt, but so did her heart. Maybe she should have met him to let him see for himself that it was over.

They could somehow remain friends. Curt might be OK with the friendship. Curt was confident in what they had. Michael's feelings might change from upset to being happy for her. What would be the harm? It couldn't hurt her again, could it? Stephanie was done hurting from her past.

Well, it was too late now. The call ended. Unless Stephanie called Michael back. She put that thought out of her head as fast as it came in.

Robert knocked at her open door as she looked up. His expression made it apparent that he knew something was wrong.

Don't Stand Still

"You didn't delete your article, did you? Are you ready for this meeting? Come on, we can't be late." Lately, when Robert noticed her upset, it had to do with something she was writing for work. Why else would she be upset? Her life outside of work was perfect. She had a beautiful home, a promising career, a best friend, and a great fiancé. "You look like you've lost your best friend, and I'm standing right here." Robert chuckled.

Reality hit Stephanie. She had always dreamed of this day, the day when Michael came back into her life. She imagined she would react just the way he did to her. But now that day was over, another thing filed in the past. The situation happened, and it was gone. He was out of her life for good. She finally had closure on the relationship. It wasn't the closure she had expected, but that chapter in her book ended.

Stephanie always hoped there were concrete reasons for why he left that she could understand. She didn't give him the chance to provide that to her. All Michael mentioned was that he wasn't ready for commitment. Stephanie had been fine with the way the relationship was moving. She thought she was punishing him for hurting her, but she just hurt herself. She may not have lost her best friend, but she felt like she lost a part of her life all over again.

Stephanie walked over to Robert. "Come on. We're late. I'm fine; my article is fine. Everything's great."

Robert stood there, looking at her.

"I'll talk to you about it after the meeting. If we walk in late, we'll get our asses chewed out again."

They walked down the hall to the conference room. Her mind raced with thoughts that were not work-related.

Everyone was in their seats with pens in hand, looking attentively at Mr. Whitam. Stephanie noticed the agenda was up as the first slide. Mr. Whitam was speaking, but she couldn't hear the words coming out of his mouth. She felts like the world was moving slowly around her, like she was in a trance. She seemed to be repeating the same steps, day in and day out. What happened to the surprise or excitement in her life? She was writing articles about movies. What happened to the tragic news?

Robert pinched her arm. She turned to look at him and noticed that everyone in the room was staring at her as well. Stephanie stood up and gave her review of the latest Richard Gere movie. The article was given excellent reviews. The statistics showed that readership was high on their website.

Robert smiled. He was always proud when she was on target when she was called on. Robert was one of Stephanie's greatest fans of her writing. He had always been the wind that pushed her further to achieve what she thought she couldn't.

The meeting concluded. Everyone rushed to get back to their desks to start working, with the exception of one person. Robert walked quietly beside Stephanie, following her to her office. As the door shut behind them, she knew to be prepared for the questions.

Stephanie said, "Do you ever feel like we're doing the

same thing every day, hour by hour? What happened to the spontaneity? Do you miss anything in your life?" These questions were directed to him, but she was trying to answer them as well. She was desperately trying to answer one question: was life more satisfying when she was happy and calm or excited and chaotic?

"You have thirty minutes to tell me what's going on before Curt gets here. You were fine earlier. If it's about work, don't even think about it. You're going on vacation soon. Take a break from here, and then you can come back with a fresh outlook. This is the best work situation we could ever have dreamed of—you and I working side by side," Robert said.

Stephanie felt bad that he was going down the complete wrong track. She could tell he was getting agitated with her, which was rare of him.

He sat in the chair in front of her desk, crossed his legs, and looked at her.

She has no choice but to come clean. She put her notebook

down. She had been looking at her notes from the meeting. When she looked up at Robert, she had tears in her eyes. "I received an unexpected call this morning from Mike. He just needed to talk, that's all. It was a short call, with little said to one another. I'm fine." She got more upset because the words didn't seem right. Were they not right because she realized her life was too much of a calm routine, or was it that she said good-bye to Michael? Stephanie was anything but fine.

Robert's tone remained even as he responded. "Steph, what did you say to him? Did you let him talk to you as he let you talk to him in the past? That's right, he never let you speak. He never returned any of your phone calls. "

"Stop it, Robert! I'm not him. Can't you see this is not easy for me?" Stephanie couldn't hold back the sobs.

"I'm sorry. Don't you remember how many nights you called him? How many times your call went straight to voice mail? All you wanted were answers. I don't want you to give him the satisfaction of speaking with him now that he's ready. Who the hell does he think he is, God? He wasn't around to provide them to you. He hurt you badly. I hate him for that. I promise you, I'll support you in whatever you do—except if it includes Michael Pellegrino." Robert knew about those long nights because Stephanie either called him or went to his house in tears. There were many nights when she fell asleep crying in his arms.

Stephanie understood why Robert was upset, but she needed to explain. "You do know you're making me feel worse. Can you give me a minute to explain before you just repeat all the obvious things I already know?" Stephanie was getting angry now.

"Sure, go ahead." Robert took a deep breath. He changed his tone to an apologetic tone.

Stephanie hesitated. "I understand what you're saying. Yes, I did let him speak. Maybe I'm a better person than he was. First he explained why he did what he did. Then he basically told me that he still loves me. He wants to get together to talk one last time. Before you stand up to react to that last statement, I said no. I told him I'm a happily engaged woman and that I'm getting married to

Don't Stand Still

Curt in a few months—which he already knew, thanks to his family. He was upset and wanted the chance to talk and explain himself." She thought before speaking again.

She was trying to determine whether to speak her thoughts out loud, not sure of the response she would get. She looked down at the floor and then spoke in a low voice, almost in a whisper. "But what if I did see him that one last time? I think it would prove to him that I'm completely over him. It's not like I'll have any other reaction than that, right? I mean he deserves to hurt as much as I did, don't you agree? If I see him, and he see's how happy I am, maybe he would feel the pain I felt every night for almost a year." Stephanie didn't know if she was trying to convince herself or Robert, but it wasn't working with Robert.

He glared at her without speaking a word, but they had a tendency of reading each other's mind. He wasn't happy her. Then he said, "You have lunch in fifteen minutes with your future husband. You need to get your head in the right place right now. You need to get your past out of your head in order to discuss your future, your wedding. Michael did nothing but hurt you. I know you have a good heart but give that good heart to Curt and Curt alone. Don't feel guilty that you're happy now. After all you went through, you deserve the happiness and joy you have in your life."

She realized he was taking it personally. Robert and Michael never had a great relationship. They both thought the other was stealing her away from them.

"You have a great, stable life right now. Curt loves you unconditionally. He would never leave you without an explanation like Michael did. If I have to remind you of that every day till the day you say, 'I do,' I will. I'm your best friend. You know I truly love you. It's my job to protect you from situations like this." Robert kissed her forehead.

God, why couldn't Robert be interested in women? That would be less complicated.

His tone grew softer. "Will you be OK? Are you going to tell Curt about this call? I don't think you should. It didn't amount to much. You know what you have to do. Keep your head up. You stood strong. You may be hurting now, but you made the right decision. I'm proud of you."

"I'll be OK."

"Of course you will be. I'm going to be leaving in a few minutes to run across the street to the bank. Call me when you come back from lunch, and we can talk more. I have your money, and when I get back, I'll leave your deposit slip on your desk underneath your keyboard." Robert stood in front of her with his hands on her shoulders, looking at her. "Have a good lunch. Try to put this behind you."

As he walked out the door, Stephanie felt even worse. She felt terrible that her anger was more toward Robert than Michael. She refused to let her emotions show. He said what he had to say. It almost felt like the conversation was dismissed. Michael had been harsh to Robert in the past. They never agreed on each other's lifestyle. But even so, Stephanie should have the right to express her feelings freely on what transpired. She felt like she didn't get a chance to say how she truly felt about the morning's encounter. Even if she was having second thoughts, this conversation with Robert would cause her to feel guilty. As she tried to organize her thoughts, the phone rang. She almost jumped out of her seat before she picked it up.

Don't Stand Still

If I keep closing and opening my eyes, maybe I'll wake

up, or maybe I'll see the face—the face of someone I

love.

—Stephanie

Chapter 9

Waking Up

The familiar voice on the other end of the phone put a smile on Stephanie's face from ear to ear. "Are you almost ready for lunch?" Curt asked. He was always prompt. It was ten minutes to twelve. He usually called a few minutes before he arrived to give her a chance to close out of things. It was a sort of courtesy call. Stephanie was happy to hear from him. She was looking forward to their lunch date.

Stephanie responded with a smile in her voice. "Yes, honey. I'm just finishing up an e-mail. How about if I meet you at the restaurant in ten minutes, unless you want to meet me here first." She paused. "Wait, why don't you do that? You never come to the office. I think it would be good for you to come here. Meet me in front of the building. I'll bring you up so you can say hello to everyone. We're asking everyone to come to our wedding. You should at least be social to them. Robert just left to go to the bank across the street. You may see him out there when you come. He could bring you up if you see him first." Stephanie was definitely the social bug in their relationship. She was the extrovert. Curt was cordial with people, but he wasn't as friendly as she hoped he would be.

Curt sighed, but, after a moment of silence, he agreed. Stephanie knew he didn't want to do this because it broke up the routine, but she hoped he could do it. The attempt to spruce things up a little would be her doing but worth it in the end. Stephanie was happy with Curt, but spontaneity in their relationship would be the extra lining.

"OK, I'll see you in a few minutes. I'm just pressing send on this e-mail, grabbing my purse and the planner, and will be right down. I need to run to the restroom fast. See you soon, babe." Stephanie hung up before Curt changed his mind. She thought about how she could bring up the phone call from Michael. She decided she would tell Curt after they ordered their food. There would be only one interruption after that when the waiter brought their order. It wouldn't be like he would be upset about it. Curt was very factual and predictable. Stephanie anticipated his response would be, "Well, you told him no, so it's done. No reason to still talk about it. Just stick to your word. Don't give him the benefit of the doubt."

On the other hand, which was hers, Stephanie might want to talk more in detail as to why Curt thought Michael called, how it made her feel, and how it made Curt feel. She stopped in her thoughts. Men usually didn't like to hear women overanalyze situations, especially if they were about men from their pasts. But this was different. It might impact them both.

Stephanie was desperate to tell someone how she truly felt about Michael calling her. She wanted to tell someone who would not take offense to it or judge her. This should be her best friend or her fiancé, but they both had a stake in it all. Robert was hurt by

Michael. Curt might not want to hear how she felt, as it might hurt him. Stephanie decided to leave it alone. She would not push either of them to talk about it. She didn't want to hurt the two men who would always be in her life. The two people who would always love her. The two people who would never hurt her.

She thought, *After lunch, I'll come back and write down how Michael made me feel when he called. What I could have said different, and what would happen if we did see each other. Venting on paper may help get everything out. That's what my counselor told me last year.*

Stephanie pressed Send on her e-mail to Dennis, closed her laptop, and grabbed her purse and planner.

She walked down the hall to the bathroom to freshen up a little and turned her cell phone on vibrate as she did whenever they went to lunch together. Curt thought it was rude to be on the phone in a restaurant. Stephanie chose to put it on vibrate rather than shut it off. As she put her phone in her pocketbook, she checked to ensure that she had her planner with all the wedding details.

Don't Stand Still

While she walked to the elevator, she realized that Robert hadn't come back from the bank yet. Maybe he ran some other errands. Maybe he was outside talking with Curt. She would talk to him when she returned from lunch to clear any doubts he had about the situation. There were really no doubts in her current relationship, except maybe some second thoughts on how she handled the unexpected phone call.

Stephanie used the elevator ride to clear her head of the past. She wanted to get to her comfort zone, which was handling tasks that were in her control. There was so much to talk to Curt about besides "the call." She had decided on the color of flowers, which limo service they would use, and who would do the readings. She wanted to go with yellow flowers. Her favorite flower was the sunflower and loved wild flowers or anything yellowish. The limo service she wanted to bring up to him was a referral from Mary. Stephanie and Curt need to discuss who would do the readings. They both had different ideas. Stephanie wanted her cousin and aunt, but Curt wanted two childhood friends. They would easily come to some type of compromise. They only had an hour and had so much to discuss.

The elevator beeped. Stephanie walked off with a few coworkers at her side. The next thing she knew, she was standing still.

People ran past her and she heard a few words: "It happened so fast," and "He didn't have a chance." She tried to get closer to the scene outside, but her feet wouldn't push her closer. She could see there were no rescue vehicles yet. This was a recent accident, something that used to get Stephanie's adrenaline pumping to try to help or to be part of the drama. This time was different. It felt closer to home. She couldn't help if she couldn't move.

Stephanie's heart stopped. She couldn't breathe. She told her feet to move, to run, and to help, but she couldn't move. Everyone was screaming and rushing to the street. It was like she was in a bubble watching this and unable to react. She just knew it is someone close to her. Why else would the pain be rushing through her? But who was it? Who was lying there in pain?

The pain struck through her heart. Her tears rolled down, and she was still short of breath. Why couldn't she see who it was? Stephanie thought, *If I keep closing and opening my eyes, maybe I'll wake up, or maybe I'll see the face—the face of someone I love.*

Don't Stand Still

Stephanie, we need some information from you.

We can start with his name and date of birth.

—Nelson

Chapter 10

Fighting Harder

"Stephanie, move!" someone screamed. "Call 911!" the office manager yelled to her. Mary ran past her and out the door. Dennis stood near the door, speaking to the security guard. Someone close to her called for help on a cell phone. He had one hand on Stephanie's shoulder and the other held the phone. She heard him speaking. "Yes, he's breathing. There's a large amount of blood loss though. I'm not sure he can move." And then he turned to Stephanie and said, "They're on their way. It will be OK."

As if the call changed everything, Stephanie walked out of the building, down the steps, to the cracked sidewalk, and into the street. The crowd was all looking at her as she pushed through

everyone with tears falling furiously. She fell down to her knees.
Then put her head on top of his chest. "Please don't go. Please
open your eyes. Squeeze my hand. Something! I'm sorry. This is
my fault." She intertwined his fingers with hers, saying a prayer
that he would be all right.

His eyes were closed, but he was still breathing. The blood
seemed to be everywhere, and his leg was definitely broken.

Stephanie knew Robert was nearby. She smelled his
cologne. It reminded her of the guilt she felt as she walked off the
elevator with the possibility that the injured person could be
Robert. *Why couldn't I go to the bank myself? Was my best friend
lying there because of me?* she thought.

When Robert walked through the door to her, Stephanie felt
relief till she looked in his eyes and knew it was someone just as
special. Robert was the one with his hand on her shoulder while
calling 911. She loved him, but she couldn't look at him. She
didn't want to look at anyone except him, lying there on the
ground.

Don't Stand Still

Stephanie didn't hear anyone talking, but they were nearby, watching, with their mouths moving. She thought she blocked all the noise so she could listen for two things: his breathing and the sirens. Stephanie wasn't sure what started or stopped first. It seemed to happen simultaneously.

The EMTs rushed toward them. One bent over his body and took vitals. They asked her to step away while they tended to him.

Stephanie started crying all over again when she was separated from him. As she moved a few steps back, she almost collapsed, but, thankfully, Robert was by her side to catch her. She put her head in his chest and cried. She didn't say a word; nor did Robert. He held her tightly, giving the only thing he could, which was his love and support. He tried to turn her away from the scene, but she wouldn't have it.

The time gave Stephanie a few minutes to think. She had lost all concept of time, but she knew it must have been past noon. She and Curt were supposed to be sitting down having fish and chips and talking about their future. She had a list of items to go over with him, such as the flowers, the maid of honor's dress that didn't fit, and their honeymoon.

Curt left all the decisions up to her, with the promise that she would go over everything with him so he had no surprises. It also made him feel included in all the decisions, even though most of them were already made. At first, this was difficult for her. Stephanie would have enjoyed making the choices with him, but she understood how busy he was at work. It wasn't that he didn't love her or didn't want to marry her. It was that he wanted to please her in any way possible. He said he enjoyed watching her plan their event. Instead of discussing these details, she was standing there with her heart broken in two. How life can change so quickly. *Curt, my love,* she thought.

Stephanie was useless to make any type of decision. She walked closer to the scene and moved away from Robert. He was hesitant to let her go. She didn't want to speak with any of the individuals she knew were staring at her. She thought they were all afraid to approach her, not knowing what to say. Stephanie tried

not to make eye contact with anyone. She wanted to be in her

bubble, away from them all, so she didn't have to answer the

questions they were eager to ask. She didn't want to have to tell

them, "I'm fine," when she knows she wasn't. Her life has been

just turned upside down in the matter of fifteen minutes. Why was

this happening to her?

She heard the EMTs speaking to each other. One said he

had a pulse. They said they needed to leave right away. The one

Stephanie noticed first on the scene, turned to her when she had

her hands covering her face as she cried. She assumed he had

noticed her engagement ring when he said, "Ma'am, I need to get

some information from you regarding your fiancé. Can you ride

with us in the ambulance?"

Stephanie responded, "Of course. Yes, I'll ride in the back

with him. Thank you." She heard Robert calling her name. She

refused to turn back now. She would call him once they reached

the hospital.

Don't Stand Still

Her manager asked Robert, "Do you think she'll be OK?"

Robert said, "No."

The ambulance doors shut. She held his hand, telling him he was going to be OK. Obviously, she didn't know if this was true, but if he could hear her, she wanted him to believe it. She said all the prayers she knew: Our Father, Hail Mary, and the Act of Contrition. "Please, God, help him," she pleaded.

Stephanie thought he squeezed her hand as she was talking about the future and the possibilities. Stephanie tried her hardest to stay positive to help him fight to stay alive. Why did this happen? Didn't he see the car? She needed to know more, but maybe not at this point in time. She refocused on him. "Open your eyes! See that I'm here with you. You're going to be fine. Just open your eyes. If you ever listened to anything I told you, let this be the one time. Open your eyes; look at me; speak to me." As she was rambling, she heard Nelson, the EMT technician, ask her for her name.

"My name's Stephanie. I know we don't know if he's

going to be OK, but I feel the need to tell him these things. Maybe

he can hear me. Maybe he'll fight harder. I have to try. I don't

want him to go. I need him to stay alive. I can't lose him. I feel like

this is my fault. He was coming to meet with me." Stephanie was

almost apologizing to him for the one-way conversation she was

having with the unresponsive patient lying in front of her.

Nelson seemed like a sincere person. He wasn't one of

those health-care professionals who didn't look people in the eye

or didn't show emotion. He responded to her in a comforting tone,

"Stephanie, I understand you're scared. We stopped the bleeding,

but we're not sure how much blood he's lost. We need him to fight

to help us work with him. If talking about your future with him

helps, then so be it. Please continue to talk to him. We're almost at

the hospital now. When we get there, I'll ask you to step out as we

transport him inside. I'll let the nurses know that you're his point

of contact. One will come out to you when she has information."

It seemed like she was about to say her farewell to Nelson.

She knew she needed to follow his directions. She didn't like that she needed to sit and be patient in the waiting room, but there was no other option. Patience was not one of her best traits.

What Nelson didn't understand was that Stephanie wasn't sure about her future. She was saying what she hoped would help him. If she had to tell him that the sky was purple to make him open his eyes, she would. She wanted the chance to apologize to him for what she had just done.

Nelson touched her left shoulder, waking her from her thoughts.

She turned to him.

He said, "Stephanie, we need some information from you. We can start with his name and date of birth."

"His name is Michael Pellegrino. His date of birth is May 13, 1971." The information flowed off her tongue as if she had known him forever.

You were my first love. You will always be my only love.

—Michael

Chapter 11

Choosing Life

Stephanie sat in the hospital waiting room. She needed to make several phone calls. The first call would be to Michael's family, but she wanted to wait to have some positive information to give them. She thought, *Maybe I should have them all come down now so we can support one another.* She was determined that when the physician walked into the waiting room, he would say "Stephanie, Michael has done great. He'll be fine." She kept counting down the minutes, hoping that in five more minutes, the doctor would come out.

Stephanie didn't attend church regularly, but she did consider herself a Catholic. She was saying the Our Father, Hail Mary, and Act of Contrition over and over. Now it was her turn to want to talk.

Don't Stand Still

She missed numerous phone calls from the office, but the more important phone calls she avoided were from Curt and Robert. Again, she felt as if she couldn't speak to anyone till she knew Michael's medical condition. She knew if she spoke to either Curt or Robert, they would ask her questions about other things than Michael's medical condition. She needed this time alone to sort things out. The guilt was overwhelming. It clouded her every thought. Stephanie felt that Michael's condition was her fault. No one could change her mind. She couldn't concentrate on anyone or anything other than Michael's well-being.

Stephanie's urgent thoughts were on Michael. What would she say to him when she saw him? Would he be OK? What was he doing there? What were her feelings for him? How could she explain them to him now in his condition? Did Michael blame her?

Stephanie took out her notebook to write down her feelings. As the pen hit the paper, she felt better, like she was talking to a friend—a nonjudgmental friend. The pen seemed to move on its own, page after page. It had always been therapeutic for her to write. She was so lost in her thoughts that she didn't hear her name being called.

Stephanie noticed an expressionless nurse walking over to her. She thought, *How am I supposed to interpret the results on this nurse's face?* Stephanie stood up and met the nurse at the entrance of the waiting room. "How is Michael? Can I see him now? Should I call his family first?" Stephanie rattled off all these questions out of nerves.

The nurse responded quickly. "Stephanie, Michael has a concussion. He is bruised up and has some stitches. Considering what happened, he is doing remarkably well. He needs his rest. Michael is a fighter. Nelson said you're his fiancé? He must have had your future in his head while in surgery." She looked like she was waiting for a response from Stephanie, but she wasn't getting one.

Stephanie stood there, silent.

"You can go in to see him for a few minutes, but, like I

said, he needs to get some rest. Understand that he may not open his eyes for a while. Your voice and words may help him. I'm sure he'll be happy to hear your voice."

Stephanie, unsure of what she would say to Michael when she saw him, just shook her head at the nurse. She hadn't seen him in years, and she was unsure of her reaction. This shouldn't have been the way the met again. "I need to call his family. I'll visit with him for a few minutes and then make my calls. Thank you so much." Stephanie grabbed her pocketbook and notebook. She took a deep breath and turned back to the nurse.

The walk to Michael's room seemed like a forever trail of the unknown—the unknown of what he would look like, the unknown of his reaction, and the unknown of Stephanie's reaction. Stephanie thought, *This will be over soon. Michael will recover. I'll visit with him to make sure he's well, and then I'll go back to my life.* This would be a short visit. Stephanie would call Curt and Robert after she called Michael's sister. Then life would be back to the way it was earlier today. Could it be that simple?

Don't Stand Still

Stephanie was in her multitasking state of mind, walking and thinking about what she would say to him in the next few minutes. She felt dizzy, probably either from nerves or from the lack of food. She just remembered she didn't make it to lunch. *Lunch! Poor Curt, he must be so confused,* she thought as she approached what she believed was the room. She was hungry, tired, scared, and emotionally drained. Soon it would be over.

The nurse opened the door and walked into the room. She turned and motioned Stephanie in. Stephanie stood by Michael's bedside, alone with him. It had been some time since she had been face-to-face with this man. Now here he was, lying in a hospital bed.

Stephanie looked closely at Michael. He looked the same except for some bumps and bruises. He still looked peaceful when he was sleeping. His hair seemed lighter than she remembered. She reached over to touch his hair lightly, but she stopped with the fear that she would wake him up.

There was a chair at his bedside. She sat next to him to be

close to him but also to balance herself. She felt a little sick to her stomach. Could be nerves. She was finally by his side again. She didn't know whether she wanted to scream or cry.

He looked as if he was sleeping peacefully. She took the time to really look at Michael's physical condition. He had a cast on his left leg and stitches above his eye, and his head had a few bandages. The sight of him made her cry. She held his hand with her head down. She put his hand on her cheek, remembering how it felt. Her tears fell down into his hand. All of a sudden, she heard one single word from Michael, "No."

Stephanie tried to compose herself quickly. She needed to be the strong one here. She grabbed a tissue to wipe away her tears and returned to the chair by his side. She looked over at him and attempted to crack a smile. "Michael, don't talk."

Immediately she said, "Wait, no, what? Are you OK? Do you want me to call the nurse?" Then she remembered the nurse reminding her that he needed his rest. "Please don't speak. She said you needed to rest. You're going to be fine. If you start talking, the nurse will come in here to tell me to leave." Without thinking, she kissed his hand.

Michael attempted to lift his arm to wipe away her one straggling tear. His eyes didn't leave hers. He had a look of concern on his face. He was lying in bed, worrying about how she was doing.

She had to let him know that she was fine, just worried. "I'm fine. I'm just happy that you're OK. You're not perfect right now, but you'll be fine. I shouldn't stay long. I need to call your family. I need to let you rest. I can come back later." Again, Stephanie rattled on. She attempted to smile, but it didn't work.

Stephanie had such a pain in her stomach. She wasn't sure if it was from hunger or from seeing Michael lying here in that state. He looked so vulnerable. He almost looked childlike holding her hand. She could feel his emotions through his eyes. She felt the passion through the way he held on to her ever so tightly. She saw the love in his eyes. She could get lost in his eyes once more, but then she thought, *Why did this man hurt me so much in the past?*

158

Don't Stand Still

Michael wouldn't let go of her hand as she tried to pull it away. She knew she needed to leave. She stayed to confirm that he would be alright, but now she didn't belong in this hospital room. Michael had a tight grip on her hand.

"Don't cry, Steph. I'm sorry." Michael paused to take a deep breath. The physical pain was evident. "At least I'm getting what I was hoping for this morning—to see you, my angel." He tried to laugh but it looked as if it hurt too much. Michael held her hand so tightly as if to say he wouldn't let her go again.

"There's nothing funny about what happened to you! What the hell happened anyway? What were you doing at my building? I told you not to come. If you listened to me none of this would have happened." Stephanie acted angry toward him to get her feelings of guilt out.

"You're as beautiful as ever, Steph. I'm sorry you have to see me like this."Michael tried to sit up in his bed but was not successful.

Don't Stand Still

"You had me worried for the last few hours. How can you even attempt to make a joke out of this? Do you know how serious it is? You're badly hurt." Stephanie refused to let any more tears escape. "I need to call your sister and your mom. Your family doesn't even know about the accident yet. I wanted to wait till I heard how you were doing. Now that I met with the nurse and came in to see you with my own two eyes, I can go call them." She attempted to get up to walk away. She was trying to be strong. She knew she needed to leave so he could rest, and she needed to call his family. This would give her time away from the situation. Walking away would be the right decision.

"Please, don't leave, Stephanie. Please." Michael's words were all jumbled. He sounded so sleepy.

As always, he had a hold on her. Hearing his voice, hearing his plea, she wasn't sure what to do. She stood still, her back toward him, looking at the door. The door represented her future on the other side. Should she choose to stay in the past or move on to the future?

Don't Stand Still

She knew the right thing to do was to make her calls, but that hold Michael had on her was too strong. She turned around and sat back down as if in a trance. Her eyes filled with tears. She felt defeated.

They looked into each other's eyes for a few minutes without speaking. Their emotions were told between their stare. They both tried to hold back the tears but equally lost that battle.

Michael held his hand out to Stephanie, and she placed her hand in his. "I'm really sorry. I am. When have you known me to take no for an answer? I couldn't have imagined today turning out like it did." He forced a smile. "I miss you. Please, let me talk."

Stephanie's thoughts were conflicting with one another, *do I walk away or let him speak after all this time?* She looked away from him and glanced down at her engagement ring. Realizing that too much time had passed to hear his plea again.

Michael didn't wait for her to interject. He wiped his tears away. "I have never stopped loving you. I have never loved anyone the way I love you. You make me whole—we make each other whole.

Stephanie interrupted, "No, if you loved me, you wouldn't have left me the way you did."

"Don't doubt my love for you. That hurts." Michael tried to reach for Stephanie's face but fell short.

Stephanie was enraged, "That hurts! I'm not sure you understand what it feels like to have your heart torn to pieces."

Michael's demeanor remained calm, "I'm sorry, Steph. I really am. I don't need anything in my life except you by my side. There's no way you've forgotten about me, or forgotten about us. I know you still have feelings for me."

Stephanie sat by his bedside shaking her head while he spoke. She had never forgotten about him and knew she would always have him in her heart. Afterall, he was her first love.

Michael went on, "I can see it in your eyes." Stephanie tried to look away. "I can feel it in your touch." She tried to pull away her hand but it was held so tightly. "We said we would love each other always. You were my first love. You will always be my only love."

Stephanie didn't understand why her heart was breaking for him after all she had gone through. "Stop, Mike. Just stop."

It was like Michael didn't hear the words Stephanie spoke, "Please. I am so sorry for what I put you through back then. I'm sorry for what I put your through today. I shouldn't have ran when I was scared. I'll regret that day for the rest of my life. A love like ours can't be duplicated. Steph, you can't deny what I see in your eyes." Bringing her hand to his lips, he kissed her fingers.

This was hard for Stephanie to digest. Michael had never spoke about his feelings so freely. She held his hand tightly in an effort to cherish the moment. Those were once the words she had wanted to hear, but not now – not anymore. She waited to hear them from him years earlier, on the day after he left and even a few weeks later. But he was right. A love like theirs could not be duplicated.

Don't Stand Still

It was nice to hear his words. Responding to him without thinking was not the correct decision, but Stephanie had no choice. "Yes, I look into your eyes, and I see the man I fell in love with years ago."

Michael interrupted, "That's right you do, I'm right here."

Stephanie looked at his smiling face as he reassured her that he was back. "I'm not done. Do I still care about you? Of course, I do. Will I ever love someone the way I loved you? Definitely not." She paused for a moment, trying to choose her words wisely. "What we had was special, or should I say different? I was obsessed with you. I couldn't breathe without you. I wanted to be with you every minute of every day.

"I still feel that way about you, Steph. Can't you see it." Michael pleaded with Stephanie.

Stephanie couldn't stop or she would lose the courage to say what she needed to say to once the love of her life. "Listen to me, I loved you so deeply that I didn't know how to love anything or anyone else, including myself. I wanted to be a part of you, which held me back from growing into the person I am today. I didn't realize all of this till you left me. I can't begin to tell you what I went through when you left. I'm sure your family told you all about it." Stephanie took a deep breath before she continued. "I didn't feel like I lost a part of me. I felt like I lost my whole self. I was desperate to find you to get you back into my life."

Michael pushed himself to finally sit upright, his physical strength overcame him emotional breakdown. "But baby, I said I was sorry. I know how wrong I was to leave you the way that I did. You were desparate to find me, now I am desparate to get you back into my life. I love you so much. Remember it was going to be only you and I, forever."

Stephanie heard not only his words but the meaning behind them. "That is the thing. It was never going to be forever, you refused to talk about forever. Then always talking about 'you and I' as if we were in a bubble away from the world. The world was still around us moving forward."

Don't Stand Still

His emotions changed, "I wasn't good enough for you? You and I had great times together."

Stephanie continued, "Yes, we had a great time together. Our laughter was like a drug. You had so much life in you." Stephanie felt stronger, but as her strength grew, so did her tears. "Without a doubt, I will never forget you. I know in my heart that I will always love you. You were my first true love. You were my first of everything. I enjoyed every day we were together—enjoyed every single moment. But that's what it was—I enjoyed the present with an unknown future. I will never forget the love we shared and I will always cherish the beautiful memories we made." She knew this was good-bye to her once believed soul mate. However, this emotional time was also the closure she needed.

She was still holding his hand and gently sat on his bed. "I don't want you to hate me, because I don't hate you any more for leaving me."

Michael was furious, "I don't want to hear it anymore! Leave!"

Don't Stand Still

Stephanie felt she needed to finish her thoughts, "I'm glad we saw each other again. I only wish it was under different circumstances. I always dreamed about seeing you and imagined what would happen. Now I know. "

Stephanie knew the words Michael spoke were out of anger as he interrupted her, "If you know now, then get out of here. I'm glad you feel good about yourself. I don't want you here any longer."

She needed to grant his wish, "I refuse to let your words hurt me. You wanted me to look into your eyes. Here I am, looking into your beautiful brown eyes. I see the man I fell in love with, but I also see the past. A great passionate past; a past I have no regrets for, a past that filled me with love. But when I look into Curt's eyes, I see our future. I see a healthy relationship. I see him and I living happily ever after with our future children by our side. I am in love with him. I'm sorry, Mike."

Michael let go of her hands. He was crushed, deflated, empty. Stephanie felt his pain but knew it was the right choice.

Don't Stand Still

"Why did you come here?" He asked through his tears. "Please, just leave. I need my rest. Thank you for coming here, but I want you to leave. Don't worry about calling my family. I'll take care of my own calls later, just leave." Michael stared blankly out the window, refusing to face her.

Stephanie was hurt by his response. Although she had suspected he would get defensive, she didn't expect him to shut down so quickly. Although her mind wandered for a moment to staying with Michael, she immediately thought about Curt again. She wanted to call him to make sure he was alright. She wanted to sit in front of the fire, cuddle up with him, and explain what happened today. It wasn't fair to keep him in suspense as long as she had.

She picked up the conversation again, "I came here because I do care about you, Michael. When I saw you lying on the ground, I felt like I was dying all over again. You were coming to see me. My heart sank when I saw you like that." She tried to hold his hand but he pulled away.

Don't Stand Still

"Don't touch me!" Michael yelled loud enough for others to hear. Stephanie was nervous that a nurse was going to walk in.

Stephanie tried to calm him down, "I'm leaving. Like I said, you'll always be in my heart. I don't want anything to happen to you. You're still a part of me, of my past. Even though you put me through hell, I wouldn't want to see you go through this. I'm sorry. I know you were coming to see me today and it felt like my fault that you had gotten hurt. I did what I thought was right by staying with you. I did what my heart told me I should do." She tried to touch his hand again but he tightened it into a fist. He refused to look at her any longer. "Please, Michael. I forgive you for what you've done to me. Your reaction like this to me doesn't seem fair. Did you think I would sit and wait for you to come back to me?"

Michael turned and looked straight in her eyes. "Leave, Stephanie!" She hadn't heard him use her full name since the first time they met, so she knew he was serious.

It was apparent this conversation was over. She didn't like

leaving him in this state of mind but had to honor his request.

Before leaving, Stephanie walked over to the other side of the bed but Michael still wouldn't look at her. She leaned over and kissed him on the head, "I will always love you, too. Good-bye, Michael." And with those closing words, she left the room.

Don't Stand Still

I know he was your first love, but I thought I was your

final love.

—Curt

Chapter 12

Loving On

Stephanie stood up against Michael's door for a few minutes, feeling numb. She felt like it was actually holding her up. She looked out to the nurse's station to see if she could locate his nurse.

She thought, *That was really hard. I hope I made the right decision. If so, why does it hurt so much? Should I go back in?* This door represented her future versus her past. She knows some of the things Michael said to her were true. She would never love anyone the way she loved him. Their love for one another was different and definitely one of a kind. But it was so intense, it was dangerous.

Stephanie took out her phone. She called Michael's sister,

Nancy, to tell her about the accident and which hospital he was in. She explained that he was doing OK physically. Stephanie had always been close with Nancy, she opened up to her about everything.

Nancy understood Stephanie's decision but couldn't hide that she was disappointed. She said, "I would love to have you back in our family once again."

Nancy said she would inform the family about Michael while she was driving over to the hospital. Before they hung up, she said, "Please keep in touch with all of us. Congratulations on your upcoming wedding."

Stephanie knew Nancy meant to keep in touch with Michael as well. The family always wanted them to reunite some day. "Thank you, Nancy. I will."

Michael's whole family was like Stephanie's second family. She decided she would leave before they showed up. It was comforting to her that they would be here shortly to spend time with him. She didn't like that he was upset, but, most of all, she didn't like that he was alone.

Stephanie felt so drained that she could collapse at any moment, although she knew she had to call Curt and Robert. She loved them both, and she knew they were probably worried sick about her. Robert probably called the hospital but couldn't get any information. He would be her second call.

Stephanie was walking to the waiting room when she felt a tap on her shoulder. She turned around to her fiancé looking at her with tears in his eyes. Curt wrapped his arms around her so tightly that she almost couldn't breathe. She tucked her head into his chest and wrapped her arms around him. They stood there for a couple of minutes that felt like an eternity. They were both sobbing, holding one another.

Once they separated, they walked hand in hand in silence to the waiting room. They sat next to each other, waiting for one to start the conversation.

Don't Stand Still

Stephanie turned in her chair to face Curt. "I'm so sorry." She put her hand on his arm. They were the only words she could get out before his tears rolled down his face, again. She had never seen him so emotional. He was usually a factual, unemotional type of person. Her heart broke again for another man.

Curt stood up. "I'll fight for you, Stephanie. I know you have a past with him. I remember you telling me about your relationship, both before and after the breakup. Yes, you had an amazing relationship with him. I feel terrible saying this now when he's in that room, injured. I don't even know the man, but what I do know is that you are mine. We're going to live our lives together—till death do us part, remember? Just because he comes back into your, or should I say our lives, doesn't mean things need to change. Right? We have plans. We love one another, right? I know he was your first love, but I thought I was your final love. I love you, Stephanie." His hands trembled as he paced around the room.

Stephanie's heart bled for him. She needed to make him

understand. She grabbed his hand to urge him to sit down next to her. "Curt, you don't understand."

He tried to stand again, but she held his hand. He tried to speak again, but he was at a loss for words.

Stephanie continued, "I'm sorry because I left you like I did without calling. I'm sorry I didn't call you right away when he called me today. I'm sorry I left you to wonder what has happening this afternoon. I'm sorry if I ever compared our relationship to mine and Michael's. But Curt, I love you. Yes, I was here with him. I felt like I needed to be with him. I'm not going to lie. I was a little confused when I was in the ambulance with him. I felt like I needed to stay by his side till he woke up. His family is on their way here. Michael will be OK. His family will support him now. We can go home."

Stephanie stopped to think through her thoughts before speaking again. *Does he need to know every detail? Should I protect him from any more heartache?* She chose her words carefully so she wouldn't hurt Curt any more than he was hurting now. "I was sitting there, holding Michael's hand, wondering what was going to happen to him. I'm not going to lie to you. He said he loved me. He came back to town because he wants us to be together again. I think I needed to hear that to see how I would react to him after all this time." Stephanie tried to hold back her tears. This had been such an emotional day for everyone.

Stephanie continued, "I do care about Michael. I think I'll always have a place in my heart for him. He was my first love. He was basically my first of everything, my first love, my first lover, and my first heartache. But I'm in love with you. I look you in the eyes, and all I see is our future, our children, and us growing old together. I look at him, and I see my past—a past I'll never regret, but that's still what it is, the past. I don't want to be with anyone but you, I promise you that. It took me this long to find my husband, my forever. I'm not letting you go." The sad tears turned into happy tears. She reached over and hugged him. Curt held her tightly. His tears rolled down his face.

Curt picked up two bags from the chair next to him.

Don't Stand Still

"What do you have with you?"

Curt placed the bags on the floor in front of their chairs. "This bag has your laptop in it, your folders that were on your desk, and your BlackBerry charger. This other bag has some snacks for you in case you were hungry. You must not have eaten today. I also grabbed your gym clothes out of your office in case you wanted to change. I thought you were maybe going to be here for a while." He reached into the bag and grabbed for something that brought the emotions back.

"I brought our wedding planner in case you needed it for anything. You left it in the restroom at your office. We were going to talk during lunch about some of the loose ends we had, like the flowers," Curt said.

Stephanie was shocked for a second. She thought she had packed it in her bag. She couldn't believe she had left it behind. She pushed the bags away and grabbed the planner out of his hands. "Yes, we have a few last minute details to go over, and then I'm ready to be your wife. How about we go home now? I'm exhausted." Stephanie stood up, put her bags over her shoulder, and began to walk away.

Curt didn't stand up at first, "But what about Michael? Are we just going to leave? Do you want to wait for his family to come? We can go to the cafeteria to have lunch if you want."

It was just like Curt to worry about others. Stephanie reassured him that Michael would be OK. He needed his rest. She explained that his three sisters, brother, and mother would be there shortly. Michael had a close family and would be in good hands.

As they were walking out Stephanie said, "It's been an emotional day. I'm looking forward to going home to a nice relaxing hot bath. I'm craving a nice, cold glass of wine. Tomorrow, I'll work on the last-minute details of the best day of our lives. First action item on my list is to contact the best man."

"Good luck with that one." Curt said. Stephanie knew it would be a difficult conversation.

Don't Stand Still

It's called control. He has always had control over your

moves.

—Robert

Chapter 13

Sharing It

Stephanie thought that it was a great idea to shut the ringer off on the phone last night. She and Curt spent a night together with no interruptions. She knew Robert would call but was also nervous that Michael might call. She knew she needed to devote her whole self to Curt for his sake and for her own.

The icing on the cake was that they both slept late for the first time in a long time. They were both so emotionally and mentally drained that they needed to sleep to reenergize for the next few weeks of their busy lives.

Stephanie woke up in a positive mood. She was ready to take on today. She poured herself a glass of orange juice and was looking out the window when Curt came up behind her. Stephanie loved the way he held her from behind and put his head on her shoulder. At that moment, she felt so loved and protected. Stephanie smiled with her fiancé behind her and her looking out to her future.

She tried to fight off the feeling of guilt she felt. She felt guilty for hurting Michael and leaving him in tears and also for what Curt went through in the last twenty-four hours. She thought about the one man who had been there for her through it all, Robert.

Stephanie grabbed for her cell phone and kissed Curt good-bye. She needed to go for a run on the beach. She put in her earphones, put her music mix on, and off she went. She ran at a fast pace as she replayed the last twenty-four hours in her head. It was amazing how intense her life had been less than a day ago.

She ran for twenty minutes along the water and then sat on the beach looking out at the calm water. She thought, *This scene— the beach and the calm water—is her perfect life. It's acceptable for life to be calm but to move forward, not standing still.*

Don't Stand Still

Stephanie sat there, smiling, and watched a man running with his dog down the beach line. Yesterday had been so emotional, but she wanted her calm back. Yes, as a child she loved the drama and basically chased after it, but she was an adult now with a grown-up life. Stephanie still wished Michael a fast recovery. She knew they would one day cross each other's path again. She felt guilty keeping Robert in suspense and worrying about her. It was time to make that phone call to him.

Her thoughts were interrupted by her phone ringing. The phone call she was expecting this morning. "Good morning, Robert."

Robert sighed. "Are you OK? What happened? How bad are his injuries? Did you go back to him? Do you know how worried I was about you? And Curt looked like he was going to collapse. Should I come over? Is Curt home with you?" Robert finally took a breath.

Stephanie knew how worried he was about her, her relationship, and her decisions. He was her best friend. They sometimes shared the same feelings. He actually sometimes felt what she felt before she did.

She understood all his questions. She loved him very much. Her life wouldn't be the same without him in it. He had been her rock for a large portion of her past. "I'm sitting on the beach while Curt is back at the house. He came to the hospital last night."

"He did!" Robert exclaimed. "What did he do? Did he go into the room with Michael?"

"No, it was nothing like that. You know Curt is more reserved than to make a scene at a hospital." Stephanie didn't know how long Curt waited for her in the waiting room. *It couldn't have been more than a few minutes*, she thought.

"I'm sorry I didn't call you," she said. "I need you to understand that I had to go with Michael yesterday. I couldn't turn around to get approval. I knew if I turned to look at you, I would have felt guilty leaving. I can just imagine the look you would have given me. I needed to make sure he was OK. He's part of my life, my past. I understand he hurt me in the end. I remember some other things as well. I sat by his side in the ambulance and held his hand. I didn't want anything to happen to him when he was coming to see me. I felt like it was my fault he was lying on the ground. Michael needed me to be there when he woke up. I needed to be with him. I was nervous that you wouldn't understand or approve.

"Curt was in my mind while I was there. I knew I needed to call both of you. I felt like something was holding me there, like a pull I couldn't resist. I needed to know what it meant." Stephanie stopped, thinking back to the conversation in the hospital room.

Robert took advantage of the pause. "A pull? It's called control. He has always had control over your moves. Do you remember that he didn't want us to be friends because I'm gay? He thought you'd catch something from me! Did he even tell you why he left? I understand he was hurt, but I hope he didn't take advantage of you because of it." Robert's tone was apparent.

"Stop right there, Robert. You and I will always be you and

Don't Stand Still

I. No one will ever come between us. It wasn't control on his part holding me there at the hospital. I wanted to be there. I needed to be there. Curt understood that when I explained it to him." Stephanie was trying not to get defensive, but she needed to keep his feelings in mind.

"I've always wanted to know how I would react the next time I saw him. Michael told me he still loved me. He wanted *us* back." Stephanie paused, long enough for Robert speak.

Robert waited for the opening, "Of course, he said he still loved you. He expected you to turn and run his way. He's not worth it. What did..", Stephanie cut him off.

"Will you wait? Please let me finish." Stephanie went on, "I knew in that moment that I would always love him, but I don't want anything other than what I have these days. I looked into his eyes, just like he wanted me to earlier in the day. I saw that those days with him and I were wild and crazy. The intenseness of our relationship, him yelling out the window, 'I love this woman,' but I also recalled him leaving me with no warning."

Don't Stand Still

Stephanie started to really believe her words. "I'm a different person now. I don't want to just enjoy today. Right?"

Robert agreed. Then Stephanie continued, "I want to plan and enjoy my future. When I look into Curt's eyes, I see something different. In our future, we have children and enjoy a stable life together. I told Michael that. My heart ached for him because I know how hard it is to lose someone you love. All this time, I think I just needed closure. I admit I'll never have a relationship like the one we had, but that's alright. I was never happy unless I was with him. That's no way to live. I need to be happy with myself before I can be happy in my relationship. Curt is everything to me, and I can't wait to be his wife. I felt so bad for Curt at the hospital. You had to see him in tears. He really thought I was leaving him for Michael." The thought of that moment gave Stephanie chills.

Robert's angered tone became sympathetic, "Of course, he thought that, poor Curt. I love you, honey."

"I love you, too. Now, hang up this phone, and get over here! We have lots to do." Stephanie started to laugh.

Robert responded, "I love you, girl. I'm so glad you are better. I'm on my way."

They hung up, and Stephanie headed back to the house.

I am physically letting you go, but, emotionally, you'll

always have my heart.

—Michael

Chapter 14

Accepting Truth

The next few weeks went by fast. Stephanie and Curt were in planning mode for the wedding. Robert jumped in to help when and where he could. She was happy that Curt and Robert blended so well.

Stephanie was making some final decisions on favors and centerpieces. Curt was leaving the choices up to her in these two areas. The wedding planner at the venue had options for her to choose from, and they were inexpensive. She didn't want to wait any longer, so she went online to make her choices. *Perfect, it's done,* she thought.

She was also keeping Robert calm about the speech he was preparing for the toast. It was comical how stressed he was. She said, "I'm the one who's supposed to be nervous, not you. Just speak from your heart. Don't read from a piece of paper. I'm not even reading my vows from notes on paper, and they're personal vows!"

They both laughed, enjoying every minute of planning this together.

Everything seemed to fall into place during the preparations for the special day. Stephanie knew it was meant to be this way. Curt was so happy, counting down the days with her. She was happy. She was in love with him, not only for her wedding day, but for her future.

Stephanie's phone rang, and she picked it up on the first ring. She dusted her desk while she was on the phone. She was constantly multitasking at work.

"Hello, to my soon-to-be wife. How's your day going? Are you ready to say good-bye to work for the next two weeks?" Curt sounded energetic on the phone.

Don't Stand Still

"Hey, you. I am so ready to leave. I'm going to lunch with Robert today and then coming back to my office to pack up. I finalized the favors and centerpieces today. I can't believe I made a change to them the day before the wedding! Anyway, I put some steak tips in the Crockpot this morning. I'll be home a little late. Can you make a side to go with it?"

"Sounds good. Well, I was just taking a break and wanted to call to say I love you. See you tonight, honey." Curt was quiet after that, but he was still on the phone.

"I know you're still there." Stephanie laughed. "I love you more." They both laughed, and she hung up the phone first. She sat at her desk smiling at the thought of how happy they made one another.

Stephanie and Robert went out for lunch. It was her last day in the office for two weeks but also the last day for lunch with him. It was such a nice day to sit outside at the café down the street. "You know I love you," she said as Robert looked down at his salad. "I'm so glad you're part of this day. Thank you for being my best friend. Thank you for accepting to be the best man. I wouldn't have it any other way."

"Don't you start getting emotional on me already," Robert said. "I love you too, honey. I'm so proud of you. You've come a long way the last few years. Curt's so good for you. I guess I approve of him. My mom will still be disappointed that we aren't getting married. I've been looking forward to this day for you." Robert's parents always hoped that they would marry each other. They didn't need to be married to love each other. They would remain friends for life.

Stephanie watched a couple walk by holding hands. She looked at Robert with less of a smile. "Is it weird that I'm not nervous? Should I be anxious? Should I be getting cold feet? I think I'm more nervous about not having all those feelings. I feel like I'm not the typical bride-to-be. Do you think I'm missing out on something?"

Robert reached for her hand. He smiled as he looked at her. "This is a how you're supposed to feel when things are right—

perfect. You're a healthy, secure, and loving relationship. It doesn't feel right to you because there are no barriers. It's a true love story, with no drama included. Enjoy it; love it; live it, honey." Then Robert looked at the couple too.

Stephanie smiled back. "Enjoy it; love it; live it. Hmm. Sounds like the perfect toast."

She always believed she and Robert would be best friends forever. She couldn't imagine her life without him. They felt each other's feelings as if they were one. Right now, she knew what he was feeling. "You're going to live your fairy tale too, you know. And I'll be the one to walk you down the aisle. You deserve as much happiness as I do. Now let's stop getting all wishy-washy. We need to head back. I have to finish cleaning my office. I'm all set with my lunch. I can't finish it all. I need to watch my weight. I have a wedding dress to fit into tomorrow." Stephanie was excited that this would be her last day in the office until she came back a married woman.

The conversation back to the office was mainly about the

wedding. They discussed how weird it would be to watch some of their coworkers dance after a few drinks. "Hey, maybe that's what they need to loosen up." Robert laughed.

When they reached her office, she turned and gave him a big hug. "See you tomorrow. Make sure Curt gets to that altar!" She kissed him and walked into her office.

Stephanie was deciding what to pack with her from her office. She knew she didn't need her project folders. Then she thought maybe just one and then chose against it. She couldn't bring work with her on her honeymoon. She packed up her notebook, laptop, day planner and pocketbook and put them by the door. Then she dusted the furniture in her office. If she had time, she wanted to rearrange the stuff on her desk.

The ringing phone startled her as she was dusting the desk around it. She thought she was silly to jump for such a minor thing, but then she knew who it was. Stephanie reached for the handset.

Mary responded, "Good afternoon, Stephanie. Getting

ready to leave for your big day? I hear it's going to be great weather tomorrow. Be sure to take lots of pictures. I'm sorry I can't come." Mary was one of the first responses to their invitations. She was going on a family vacation over the weekend.

Stephanie interrupted Mary before she went on about her weekend adventure. "Thank you. Do you have someone on the line for me?"

"Yes, I do. Sorry about that. I have a gentleman on the line for you. I'll transfer him right over. Have a great day." Mary transferred the call.

Stephanie felt bad for being short with Mary, but she wanted to ease the feeling she had in the pit of her stomach. She knew who it was even before he said a word. She remembered how Michael would be standing behind her out of the blue. She didn't even need to turn around; she knew he was there.

One day, Robert and Stephanie went out for the night. They stayed at a bar till closing. When they were leaving, Stephanie looked down and noticed a third shadow. She didn't need to turn around. She knew who it was. It was the same feeling she had at this moment.

"I hear the time has come for you to walk down the aisle. I didn't get a chance to thank you for staying by my side at the hospital. I'm sorry I was so angry with you before you left. Maybe it was the drugs they had me on. I guess it sounds weak of me to blame the drugs on my childish, selfish behavior. I was wrong to be angry." Michael stopped to wait for a response. All he got was dead air. "I'm not calling to say or do anything crazy. I promise. I just wanted to wish you my very best. I'll be thinking about you tomorrow."

Stephanie took a deep breath. "Thank you. How are you feeling? How long were you in the hospital for?" She thought it was weird that she really did care how he was feeling. But then she retraced her thoughts *Michael has been part of my life for a while. I just want to hear he's doing well. There's nothing wrong with my concern.*

Don't Stand Still

"I'm doing well. I was in the hospital for six days. Six days too long in my opinion. I need to look both ways when I cross a street from now on." They both laughed. "Boy was that a surprise. Here I was going to say hello to an old friend. It's like God was trying to stop me in my footsteps. He was telling me to leave things alone. The car definitely stopped me, huh?" Michael laughed.

Stephanie interrupted. "That's not funny. You scared us all. You were just lying there, not moving. When I was young, my adrenaline used to get pumping when accidents happened. Not that I wanted to see anyone hurt, but I wanted to report it. But it's different when it's someone you—" Stephanie stopped in her tracks. "Someone you care about. It was a sight I won't get out of my head for a long time. Just knowing you were on your way to see me, and then this happened. It was heartbreaking. I'm glad you're doing well now though. I'm sure your family took good care of you."

Stephanie paused for a second. "So why the surprise phone

call today? You're driving the receptionist crazy, calling in on at that line." She felt more at ease. She hoped Robert wouldn't walk in, since she wanted to finish this discussion.

Stephanie looked around her office, knowing everything was done. She was ready for her vacation to begin. She didn't mind taking a few minutes to chat with an old friend. She was trying to justify the reasons to stay on the call. It was wrong, but it felt right.

"Well, I don't want to take too much of your time. I know that tomorrow's your big day. I don't want you to have any stress the day before your wedding. That's not the reason for this call. I won't be there to sing "Lady in Red," well, for obvious reasons, such as that you'll be in white." He laughed. He sounded so calm and relaxed. She wasn't sure what she was expected from him, but it definitely wasn't the calm, at-ease tone he was displaying.

Stephanie wondered where Michael was. Was this for real, or was he trying to convey a secret message?

Don't Stand Still

Michael continued. "I'm happy for you, Steph. I'd love to somehow still be in your life but know that's probably not possible. So I was thinking of a way that I can silently be there for you on your most special day." He stopped.

"Oh dear. Mike, what are you talking about now? Please, don't do anything crazy. Can you see my parents faces if they saw you tomorrow!" Stephanie laughed. This felt like a conversation with a friend. She wasn't nervous or uneasy, just guilty for enjoying it.

"Nothing like that. I wouldn't do that to you or your family. Or Curt. From what I hear, he's actually a good guy. But tomorrow morning, when you put on that beautiful gown, I want you to know that I think you look gorgeous. As the limo is picking you up, know I'll be around to catch a glimpse of you walking out of your house. As you walk down the aisle, I don't want you to have any fears that I'll interrupt the wedding but know that I'll always love you. Remember our song, "That's What Love is All About"? It's about letting go. If you ever have a bad day, I want you to think back of some of those crazy things we did when we were young. Remember the time you found me in our hotel room sitting in the tub with my beers? You were furious at me but wouldn't let it show. We had some funny times. I want them to bring you up when you're down. Those times still make me laugh, smile, and feel at ease." Michael seemed to be trying to hold back his emotions, but it was obvious how he was feeling.

"Curt is a lucky man. He has my beautiful angel girl who I loved from the day I met her. I want more than anything in the world for you to be happy. I know he makes you happy. You always wanted to move forward. I lived in the moment. *We* lived in the moment. This is my moment, my moment in time where I'm telling you I will always love you. I'm going to do the hardest thing I've ever done in my life, and that is to walk away. I'm physically letting you go, but, emotionally, you'll always have my heart." Michael stopped.

Stephanie was in tears over his beautifully chosen words. "Where did this sweet Mike come from? Where's comical Mike?"

Don't Stand Still

She tried to laugh to try to ease the tension. "Seriously, I want you to be happy too. Thank you for calling and for making me feel special. You and I definitely did live in the moment. I don't think I remember one day when we didn't have fun. Yes, we had our arguments, but we laughed about them by the end of the day. It was hard sometimes to date a comedian, someone who always wanted to make everyone laugh. I was so jealous. I didn't want to share you with anyone. You'll always be in my heart as well. I do think about you often." She immediately regretted her words. "I should get going."

"This isn't good-bye. Good-byes are too depressing. Take care of yourself, Stephanie. Follow your dreams where ever they may lead you. Remember, I'm like your guardian angel. I'll always be watching over you, thinking of you, wishing you well, bringing you up when you are down by our memories, and loving you. Always. See you later, sweetie." Michael hung up the phone.

Stephanie sat in her office for a long time. She would keep this conversation to herself, at least till after the wedding. She didn't want to stress Curt or Robert out. It wouldn't hurt if she never spoke of it to anyone.

She thought about everything they said. What did it all mean? *It means that Michael is moving on but will always care for me*, she thought. Stephanie could accept that concept. But how did she feel about the words they exchanged? Michael conveyed some strong words to her. It ended up getting comfortable talking to him.

They laughed together on the phone, just like old times. She thought, *Maybe one day—not for a long time, but some day— we could be friends again.*

Stephanie overanalyzed the conversation. The conversation made her happy in a weird way. She thought, *It's not like I'm cheating on Curt. It's just admitting that we're moving on but will always care for one another. So he's looking after me. He'll be thinking of me. You can never have too many guardian angels, right?*

You are the best thing that has ever happened to me. I

love you to the moon and back.

—Stephanie

Chapter 15

Embracing It

Stephanie smelled the steak tips from the back deck. When she walked in, the dinner table was set. Curt stood there with a glass of wine in hand.

"I can't drink the night before my wedding." She laughed as she took a sip of the wine.

"It's one glass. When I leave, I expect you to drink just water and go to bed early." They both laughed. Curt walked served the food in the plates. "How was work today? I pray you decided not to take any work home with you."

"I left it all there. Just took my notebook and laptop. I had to take something with me in case my husband gets bored with me. Do we need to research what fun things to do on our honeymoon."

Don't Stand Still

Stephanie smiled as she looked up at Curt.

Curt kissed Stephanie on the back of her neck. "Bored? We'll be anything but bored." Kissing her ear, Curt lowered the kiss back down her neck. "Are you still adamant about tonight? Do we still have to behave? Are you still throwing me out?" Curt sat down across from her.

Stephanie took a deep breath before speaking. "If you keep doing that I may change my mind." She didn't want to give into her desires right now. She needed to be strong.

"Wow, this tastes so good," Stephanie said as she took a bite of her meat. "I'm sorry, I couldn't help it. It smelled so good. Yes, darling, you will be leaving after dinner. I may let you stay for a little while longer, but off you go." She wanted the night before her wedding to be traditional. She was planning on having some good quality alone time.

They made small talk as they finished their dinner. Stephanie felt guilty about her earlier conversation with Michael. She didn't like to keep secrets from Curt. The conversation doesn't affect her relationship with him. She was still happier than ever, and she couldn't wait to walk down the aisle to start her life as a married woman.

She stood up to clean up after dinner.

Curt came up behind her, placed the dishes in the sink, and put his arms around her. He lifted her head to look at him. "I love you. I can't wait till tomorrow." His kissed her on the nose and then leaned down and kissed her lips. They stood there for a while, just kissing and holding each other. "I promise tomorrow will be perfect."

"It won't be anything but perfect with you by my side. Unless our crazy families dance on the tables." Stephanie laughed at the thought. "Seriously, I'm not even nervous. Maybe tomorrow morning I'll be stressing out, but it's been a great experience to plan. I didn't want to be one of those brides who worries about each detail of the entire day. I just want to be married to you and enjoy the day."

Don't Stand Still

"Can we practice one thing tonight before I leave?" Curt let her go and walked to the living room.

"What are you doing?" Stephanie walked over to Curt.

He took her hand and swung her around. Then the music started to play. "Amazed" by Lonestar was their wedding song.

"Let's practice our first dance." Curt held Stephanie tightly. She felt all the love, passion, and happiness in him, and she felt the same way. They danced for a few songs till it was time to go their separate ways.

"You are the best thing that has ever happened to me. I love you to the moon and back." Stephanie said as she said good night.

Don't Stand Still

Enjoy it; love it; live it.

—Robert

Chapter 16

The Wedding Day

Stephanie woke up feeling slightly guilty for not telling Curt about her conversation with Michael. The conversation made her feel good. But then she looked at her wedding gown hanging on the door and knew she didn't want anything to ruin this day. She wanted it to be perfect.

Stephanie enjoyed the silence in her house. She could actually hear her heart beating. She had a full day ahead of her. Why not enjoy the little bit of time she had alone? She made a light breakfast, thinking that if she didn't have anything big to eat, she wouldn't have any stomach issues. She had chronic stomach issues, but she didn't want that to interfere in their day. Cranberry juice and a corn muffin was her perfect fast breakfast.

Don't Stand Still

She called her mom before she started the items on her to-do list. "Good morning, mom. How's it going over there?"

"Everyone's awake. We probably won't start getting ready for a bit. Your dad slept late this morning. I'm making him some breakfast now. Are you getting nervous? Did you eat?" Stephanie could hear her mom moving around the kitchen.

"I'm not nervous yet. Curt came over last night for dinner, and he went home probably around nine. I think he's more nervous than I am. I'm having a muffin now. Tell Dad I love him, and I'll see him soon. I'm second-guessing myself that I should have slept at your house last night. I'm enjoying the quiet, but I feel like I should be running around with everyone." Stephanie felt uneasy about being so relaxed.

"You'll start running around soon. Just remember to enjoy the day. It goes by fast. Love you. I'm going to finish breakfast for your father." Stephanie's mom was great at taking care of everyone in the family.

"OK, Mom. Love you more!" Stephanie hung up the

phone.

The first item on her agenda was to take a shower. She made it a long, cleansing shower. The shower is where she thought most of the time. She thought about her to-do list, thought up new articles to write, and she even decided most of her Christmas list. It was her time.

Today she thought about walking down the aisle to the man of her dreams to begin the rest of their lives. It made her smile. She remembered just in time that the hairdresser told her to make sure that her hair was not freshly washed before her appointment.

Everything was laid out on the bed: her sweatpants, white button-up shirt, and her flip-flops. She turned once more to look at her gown hanging on her door. After her hair and makeup were done, her final step would be to step into the beautiful, elegant gown. Stephanie started getting dressed as her doorbell rang. She got her shirt and underwear on before walking to the door.

"You're not ready yet? It's your day. This is so exciting! What else do you have to do?" her sister Alicia said.

Don't Stand Still

"We brought you breakfast—a corn muffin and tea. It shouldn't be too much for your stomach. Did you already eat?" her sister Angelica said.

Her sisters sat on the couch as Stephanie ran to put on her sweatpants and flip-flops. She reentered the room feeling more relaxed than ever now that her sisters were by her side. They would get their hair done at the same salon. Everything seemed to be falling into place.

"Where's Mom? Thanks for breakfast. I just had a corn muffin. I'm so afraid to eat. With all my stomach issues, I'll probably end up in the bathroom all afternoon. Imagine that! 'Excuse me. Can we put a hold on the vows while I run to the bathroom?' I'll take that tea though. We still have a little time before we need to leave for the hairdressers."

Angelica responded, "I'll eat the corn muffin then."

Stephanie laughed. Her sisters just looked at her, smiling.

Alicia broke the silence. "Mom wasn't quite ready. She was helping Dad all morning in the shower. She was getting his suit on and then his shoes. She has her hands full getting him all set. She should be ready shortly. She decided to do her own hair rather than having it done at the salon. I told her that you wouldn't mind. You know how particular she can be with her hair." She paused. "Stephanie, don't look at me like that. Let mom enjoy today too. At least she's not rushing around."

Stephanie was a little disappointed that her mom wasn't with her but knew the whole family would be together shortly. She thought, *This day is going to be perfect. Nothing will interrupt it* to help ease the stress that was finally setting in. "I need to put my dress, shoes, and everything in the car. Angie, can you grab my makeup case from the bathroom? I'll grab the dress and shoes."

Stephanie picked up her dress, shoes, and accessories. She took one look around the room and smiled. Then she yelled out to her sisters, "OK. Let's head out and get this day started."

The girls packed the car with the needed items. Everything seemed to be moving slowly. Stephanie was a little anxious but didn't want to mention it to her sisters. They would ask questions and discuss why she felt that way. *It's a normal feeling on such an important day. Curt is probably feeling the same way,* Stephanie thought.

As they left for the hairdresser, Stephanie looked everywhere, but there was no sign of anyone suspicious. The drive was entertaining, and it helped with the nerves. This was exactly what she needed—quality time with her sisters. They had all the old hip hop songs on in the car, and the girls all sang to each other.

They were in the hair salon for almost two hours. A hairdresser was assigned to each of them. Stephanie made sure there were water bottles, Mimosas, and fruit for them to snack on. It was designed to pamper them.

Angie and Alicia both went straight to get their hair done. They wanted their hair to be half up and half down. Stephanie went to get a pedicure and a manicure. She couldn't believe how fast both were completed. When she sat in the chair to get her hair worked on, her sisters sat by her side. They were beautiful. Alicia was enjoying her second glass of mimosa, and Angie drank a bottle of water and ate fruit while watching Stephanie's hairdresser.

Stephanie loved how her hair looked with the veil. She wondered if she would be able to keep the veil on all day. There were so many pins and so much hair spray in her hair that she didn't think it would move much.

Stephanie didn't ask her sisters to have their hair any certain way. "You both look gorgeous. Wow! Hot mamas! Thank you so much." The first sets of tears trailed down her face. She knew there would definitely be tears today, but she didn't think it would happen so soon.

"You look like the beginning of a beautiful bride. I love your hair. You definitely picked a style that matches you." Angie stood up and handed Stephanie a tissue. "Don't you start crying now."

It was the perfect time to start crying. Her last step at the salon was her makeup. The girls did their own. Stephanie's hairdresser, Sam, knew exactly what Stephanie wanted.

"OK. Makeup…check. Hair…check. Nails…check.

Mimosa…check. And now, what's next?" Stephanie looked over to her sisters, giggling like a schoolgirl. She was enjoying the pampering. She hadn't spent this much time alone with her sisters in a long time.

Alicia said, "Let's head over to Mom's to finish you off with your gown,". She then laughed before she started up again "You can't get married in sweat pants, right? Now if we were talking about Angie that would be a different story!" Wearing sweatpants was something Angie would definitely do. Alicia opened the hairdresser's door for Stephanie. They walked over to the car, and Alicia handed the keys to Angie.

The day was going as smooth as Stephanie dreamed it would. She was at ease, spending quality time with her family before she walked down that aisle. Things always seemed to feel normal, safe, and comfortable with "her people." Stephanie wondered whether she should call Curt or not. She chose against it. She wanted him to miss her. She wanted him to look forward to watching her walk through the door at the church.

Don't Stand Still

Angie parked the car in the driveway. Alicia jumped out first since she needed to use the bathroom, while Angie waited for Stephanie to get out.

Stephanie opened the door to step out of the car and almost tripped. "I'm so clumsy. Better to trip now rather than later right?" They continued walking into their parents' house when Stephanie stopped. "I'll be right in. I just need a minute."

Angie walked in the house and left Stephanie behind. She stood on the doorstep, facing the door to the house. The feeling was so strong, she couldn't help but turn around. Michael sat in his car in the parking lot across the street from her parents. Stephanie wasn't going to walk over to him or wave. It was enough to know that he was there. She had known she would either see him or hear from him somehow. He was just sitting there, not making a move. She made sure he noticed her looking his way. They definitely made eye contact. Stephanie smiled his way. After a minute she walked into the house.

"Mom, Dad, you ready to give your daughter away today?"

Stephanie said as she walked into the house. She was so happy.

She was happy about marrying the man of her dreams, but that one

moment outside her parent's house meant something to her. She

would always care for Michael, as she now knew he felt the same

way. But life moved forward. She almost felt as if she had the

whole world right in front of her.

"Time is ticking. What were you doing outside? We need

to start getting you ready." Stephanie's mom said as she walked

over to admire Stephanie's veil.

"I'm here; I'm here. I just needed some fresh air. I needed a

minute after Angie's driving." Stephanie hit Angie's arm.

Alicia was already dressed. Angie was just finishing

another bottle of water. *Angie would be the one to make everyone

late*, Stephanie thought. "Angie, will you please start getting

ready?"

Stephanie took a good look at her mom. She was gorgeous.

Her dad looked as handsome as ever. "You both look great. I have

the best-looking parents ever." She was so lucky to have both her parents by her side today.

It was her turn to put on her dress.

Her mother walked over to Stephanie. "I'm so happy for you. This day will be so special for you and Curt. Don't forget to go over to each table at the reception and thank each guest for coming. Don't forget to eat your dinner. Also, don't forget to smile for all the pictures. Most of all, don't forget you'll always be our little girl."

Flood works started for everyone in the house. Stephanie's mom leaned over and embraced her in an emotional hug, almost as if either one did not want to let go. They both felt the love between each other. They were like best friends.

Angie walked out of the bedroom in her beautiful dress. "What is going on? Today is a happy day, everyone! Why isn't she even dressed yet? You're all making me stressed." She was the comic of the bunch.

Stephanie walked into the bedroom and closed the door behind her. Then she opened it up a crack. "Aren't you all coming in to help me?"

Her sisters laughed and walked in behind their mom. "Dad, you need to wait."

Stephanie walked into her dress as her mom zippered the back of it. She attempted to sit on her mother's bed to put on her shoes, but it didn't work that well. Her sisters had to put on her shoes. She felt like a princess. She panicked when she couldn't find her jewelry, but Alicia came to the rescue. "Here's your necklace and earrings. I think someone's getting nervous."

"I am not," Stephanie responded. "I think we're running late. Mom, did you eat? What else do we have to do?" She asked a lot of questions when she was nervous about something.

"You look beautiful," Stephanie's mom said with a smile. "I think the only thing left to do is relax. The photographer should be here in less than fifteen minutes. The limo will be here in forty five minutes. All the flowers are here, ready for us. Let's go out there. Are you ready to show your dad his little girl?" She opened the bedroom door and walked into the kitchen.

Don't Stand Still

Stephanie's dad was smiling from ear to ear. He was as sentimental as she was. He had tears in his eyes as he looked at his youngest daughter in her wedding gown. Stephanie always looked up to her father as her hero. She always envisioned marrying someone like him: affectionate, loving, and caring as her dad was with her mom. She walked over to him and leaned down to kiss him on the cheek. "Hi, Daddy. How do I look?"

Her father's response was short and sweet. "Like a princess, my peanut."

Everything seemed to be happening so fast. The photographer arrived and took pictures of all of them. Every pose, every combination: father and daughter, mom and daughter and so on. The photographer was patient. Stephanie wanted pictures in the house. She wanted pictures outside in the backyard. She wanted pictures getting into the limo. He captured everything she envisioned. He reassured her that his partner was with Curt taking all the pictures she wanted with him.

The limousine showed up shortly after the photographer

completed what seemed like two hundred photos. Stephanie felt

anxious. She wanted to get to the moment when she saw her future

husband.

When it was time to walk out of the house to get into the

limousine, Stephanie thought, *I wonder if he's still sitting outside*

in his car. Should I go out to check before everyone else goes out?

He promised not to do anything crazy on this special day. Her

parents and Alicia walked out first, with Angie walking behind

Stephanie.

Stephanie did a fast look, but Michael was nowhere in

sight. *Good, I didn't want him to see me in my gown. I hope he's*

not at the church, she thought.

Everyone got into the limousine included Stephanie. "I

didn't think I'd be able to get into the limo with this huge dress. Is

everyone in? Mom and Dad, you both look great. Are you

comfortable? It's nice in here, right?" The inside of the car was

nice. There were lights on the ceiling and a TV on the side. Angie

started playing with the gadgets and put some music on for the ride.

"Thanks," Stephanie said. "I think the music will distract my nerves. Ugh, why am I nervous? I've been fine all day. I didn't want to be a nervous bride. I went all this time remaining calm, and, now, look my hands are sweating."

"You'll be fine," Stephanie's mom responded putting a hand on her knee. "It's a good nervous feeling, right? You're excited for this day. You've always dreamed of this day growing up. I'm surprised you didn't have it all planned before someone even asked you to marry him."

Everyone in the limo laughed, including Stephanie. She actually did a report in high school on planning a wedding. It included a guest list, favors, venue, centerpieces, and the budget. She kind of did plan her wedding before, even if it was just for school.

They were now on their way to the church. "I think you're right, Mom. No, I know you're right. I'm just anxious. Everything will be perfect. I'll be fine as soon as we make it to the church. So, do you think it was the right choice for us to write our own vows? We both like short and simple. That's why we decided to try to do it on our own." For the first time all day, Stephanie's stomach started to bother her.

"You'll be fine." Her father chimed into the conversation.

"Yes, you'll be fine," her sister Alicia said. "Did you print them out? You must have practiced them a hundred times. Just remember, look into Curt's eyes. Do not look down at the paper. When you're speaking to him, try to remain calm. Do you want to read them to us now?"

"I didn't write them out. I'm going to speak from the heart, and I've memorized what I want to say." Stephanie responded to Alicia.

Alicia gaped at her. "You didn't write them out!"

"Oh, Alicia, don't look at me that way. Now I'm nervous. You think I should have printed them. I'll be fine. Once the ceremony is done, we get to relax."

They all looked at her, but, before they could respond, her mother's phone rang. She smiled at Stephanie after she answered. "Hi, sweetheart…Yes, she is. We're on our way…Of course you can, one second. Maybe you can calm her nerves a bit." Her mom handed Stephanie the phone.

Stephanie took the phone, hoping Curt was as anxious as she was.

"Were you expecting someone else?" Robert asked. "You realize it's against the rules to talk to your fiancé till you reach the altar, right? I'm not a rule breaker as much as I look like one." He laughed. "How are you doing? I thought you were going to send me a photo of you in your gown. I see my needs no longer matter."

"I'm doing OK. We're driving your way now. I decided you'll see me when everyone else does. Seriously, when you see the limo pull up, sneak on over!" Stephanie relaxed more. "How's Curt? Does he seem nervous to you? Is everyone behaving? Are you at the church yet? Are all the guests there?" Stephanie picked at her dress while she waited for his response.

Don't Stand Still

"Everything's fine. Curt's fine. He seems as cool as a cucumber. The guests are showing up now," Robert responded.

Stephanie listened to the noise in the background.

"Curt and a few of us just had a beverage in a small, tiny glass." Robert laughed. "Don't worry. We'll see you in a few minutes."

"Robert, don't you let my fiancé get drunk on our wedding day. Promise that is the last one he has. Relay that message to my brother, too," Stephanie said. "OK, we'll see you soon. Love you too." Stephanie handed the phone back to her mom. "I feel like I'm getting hives on my neck. Do I look all right? Am I all red and blotchy?"

"You look stunning, honey. If you don't scratch it will go away. Leave it alone. You'll be fine. You're getting me nervous. Everything will be fine." Her mom put her hand on Stephanie's shoulder. "Breathe. The day will be beautiful. Nothing can interfere with such a wonderful day as today."

Stephanie hoping nothing—or no one—would. She hoped

her nerves were because she was anxious to get the day started, and not about any uninvited guests showing up.

The limo approached the church. Some of the guests were walking into the church. Stephanie had the urge to get out of the limo to greet everyone, but knew she had to wait. The driver walked around to open the door for her sisters and her parents. When her father stepped out, the driver shut the door.

It flew open again. Stephanie's heart almost dropped. Standing before her was her best friend. He jumped in the limo by her side. "Darling, you look beautiful. I know I don't have the full view yet, but you look like a princess." Robert had tears in his eyes. "Do you need anything from me?"

"I need to stop shaking. I feel like I'm going to have an anxiety attack." Tears filled Stephanie's eyes. "I know I'll be fine by the time I get into the church."

Robert wiped away one lonely tear on her cheek. "Your sisters will kill me if you ruin your makeup. You'll be fine. Just look right at Curt while you walk down that aisle. If you look at my mom, she'll try to make you laugh." He held her hands. "This is the beginning of the best day of your life. Enjoy it, love it, and live it!" He kissed her and left.

Stephanie was alone in the limo for a few minutes. She took a few deep breaths, and then the door opened once again. Her father was waiting for her with his hand out. Stephanie placed her hand in his. There were flashes from a few different cameras. She felt like she was in the middle of all the paparazzi. She remembered to smile when she walked out of the car. She was prepared for the cameras.

The wedding party walked into the front of the church to line up. As Stephanie walked in, she realized she hadn't looked around outside to see if *he* was out there. It didn't seem to matter. All that mattered to her was walking down the aisle to stand before God and say her vows to her future husband.

Robert and Stephanie's brother, Vincent, walked over to her. Vincent, who didn't normally show his emotions, kissed her on the cheek and gave her a hug. He then went to stand by their mom's side.

Robert had tears in his eyes as he looked at her. "You really do look like a princess, girlie. Your fairy tale is about to begin." He wiped away a tear and then continued. "I love you so much. Curt is so happy right now. I don't blame him one bit. He's marrying the smartest, most beautiful woman I know." He kissed her on the cheek. "Now, don't you start crying, or you'll mess up your makeup."

Stephanie smiled and squeezed Robert's hand tight. "I love you." She couldn't have come this far without him by her side. He held her up during lows when she would have crashed if he hadn't caught her.

Stephanie got nervous when she heard the music. Vincent walked their mom down the aisle and then came back. Stephanie chose not to have a large wedding party, which was perfect for her. Vincent walked down the aisle with Angie, Robert walked down the aisle with Alicia, and then there was her.

The butterflies flew around in Stephanie's stomach. She

concentrated on not getting sick. She kept repeating to herself, *It's going to be OK*. The doors to the church closed. She knew that meant she and her dad were next.

Stephanie looked at her dad. "Don't let me fall. Don't walk too fast. I love you." She felt like she was reunited with her daddy from when she was young. He looked so happy. She was so happy to have him to walk her down the aisle. She felt blessed to have him by her side for the few minutes before she was to be married.

Her dad leaned over to her and, in a whisper, said, "I love you too, peanut." He put his arm through hers, holding her tight. "Let's go."

The doors swung open. She heard the infamous "Here Comes the Bride." Stephanie walked one step at a time with her dad. She didn't look left or right at the guests, she looked straight ahead. She was so focused on the altar where Curt was standing. The walk seemed to be a mile, even though it was only a few steps away.

Her dad stopped in front of Curt. He shook Curt's hand and

then kissed Stephanie before walking away.

Curt and Stephanie both said, "Hi," to one another as they held hands and looked in each other's eyes. The moment felt so right.

The priest welcomed the guests. Curt and Stephanie looked at one another like there was no one else in the room but them for the whole ceremony.

They were brought out of their trances when the priest said the word *vow*. Curt took a piece of paper from his pocket. Stephanie cringed, feeling terrible that she didn't write hers out.

Curt opened the paper and took a deep breath before beginning. "Stephanie Ferrari, I know I haven't said some of this to you before. I want to explain something to you now, in front of our family and friends. I never believed in luck, miracles, or fairy tales. But from the moment you stepped into my life, I felt like you were my miracle. Before you entered my life I felt like I had it all—a stable job, a fulfilling career, and a great support system. But I didn't have anyone to share it all with. Then you walked into my life as carefree as you always do. I knew from the moment I met you that you were the one. You were the one I wanted to wake up to each morning and the one I wanted to share my life with, day in and day out. You were the one I wanted to grow old with. You were the one to be my best friend and wife in one." Curt stopped to take a breath.

"I will laugh with you when you're happy, I will cry with you when you're sad, and I will be angry when you are angry. You are my sunshine and my moonlight. Today, I want to say thank you for coming into my life and committing to staying in my life forever. I promise I will try to be as perfect as I can be for you. I love you today and always." Curt's happy tears fell down his cheeks. He leaned over and kissed Stephanie lightly on the lips. Then he looked over to Stephanie's parents. They had tears in their eyes as well.

Stephanie was nervous. She had no paper to look down at, nothing to hold in her hands.

Curt looked surprised that his organized fiancé didn't have

any index cards to refer to.

She knew she needed to hold on to something, so held out both her hands to him. She took a deep breath.

"Curt, thank you. I don't think I can top that." Stephanie laughed and squeezed his hands. "No one has ever made me feel the way you do when I'm with you. You make me want to grow. You make me feel like I can do anything I put my head and heart into. You inspire me with your drive on life. I love you today and will love you each day of our lives. You are my world. I don't want to stand still. I want to move forward with our lives as one, starting today. We're good together. No, we're great together. I hope you will have me even though my imperfections show from time to time. But I promise you as well that I will try to be as perfect as I can be for you. I love you."

Stephanie was glad they chose to say their own vows. She and Curt played with the word *perfect* for months. They joked with each other, stating that they were not perfect. They both decided to use it in their vows. But what stood out was that Stephanie didn't want to stand still any longer. She wanted to move forward to a future with her husband, Curt.

The fairy tale she dreamed of was now in her grasp. They would live happily ever after, as that is how all fairy tales are supposed to end.

Don't Stand Still

Don't Stand Still

About the Author

JoAnn Scanlon was born in Providence, Rhode Island, on March 19, 1973. As the youngest of four children, she watched her father work two jobs and her mother raise the household as a stay-at-home parent until JoAnn reached her middle-school years. In her own words, "We may not have been from a wealthy family, but we were rich in family love."

JoAnn went to Classical High School in Providence, Rhode Island, and, a few weeks after graduation, began working at her first full-time job. She ended up staying there and attending university night classes over a seven-year period. In 1997, she met her husband, Kevin Scanlon, and, a year later, transitioned careers and pursued a position in customer service. After a short period, JoAnn was promoted to customer service manager and later went on to lead multiple teams within the service industry. These days, JoAnn has embraced yet another career change as manager of communications.

In 2000, JoAnn and Kevin married. In 2005, after numerous attempts to start a family, they welcomed their beautiful son, Tyler. In 2007, against even more odds, the Scanlons gave birth to a second boy, Nicolas. In JoAnn's words, "Family life is the most important thing to us. My dream was to be a stay-at-home mom, but I knew that financially, we both needed to work to provide our boys a wonderful childhood."

Throughout the years, JoAnn found herself dreaming up ideas for novels of all genres: drama, suspense, mystery, and romance. "I am definitely a daydreamer," she states. "There were times that I would actually daydream the oh-my-God moments of a book and would have tears rolling down my face because of something that happened in the book." After years of creating these fictional stories in her imagination, JoAnn decided to pursue her true passion: writing. Why couldn't it be done?

Today, JoAnn wants to instill this same value of exploration in her children. "I want to teach my boys that you can try anything. If you break down any goal into a list of tasks, it will turn into an achievable goal. Start off by handling the smaller tasks and move on to the larger items."

Do or do not…there is no try. —Jedi Master Yoda.

Turning daydreams into words.

—JoAnn Scanlon

Made in the USA
Middletown, DE
26 July 2015